Everything about this man was perfect from his dark brown, perfectly cut hair to his impeccably tailored suit.

There was not a strand out of place. It was as if even dust had deemed him too powerful to sully.

He certainly wasn't local. Gisele would have remembered him and the way her stomach was currently somersaulting. Instead of assisting him she was picturing what his embrace would be like! How could he cloud her mind like that just by stepping into her shop? "Can I help you?"

She noticed his pupils flare as she spoke, then he cleared his throat, lightening the gravel just a touch. "I'm certain you're the only one who can."

The way he looked at her made the flower shop shrink in size. The air became thicker.

"What's the occasion, and what sort of arrangement are you looking for?" She reached beneath the counter and pulled out a notepad and pen so she could write down as many notes as possible about his order.

"The event is a wedding, and the arrangement is a mutually beneficial one."

Enter the glittering kingdom of Alouette
in this dramatic royal trilogy by Bella Mason!

Scandal at the Palace

They're writing history...in red-hot ink!

In Alouette, the royal name of *Bettencourt*
means privilege, luxury, power... And yet for
Crown Prince Claude and his sisters,
Gisele and Isabelle, born into a life of isolation
and crushing pressure, their elite status
is little more than a gilded cage.

But romance—and revolution—
are in the air... Alouette's about to see that passion
doesn't play by palace rules!

Princess Gisele fled the palace rather than bow
to her parents' control. But irresistibly ruthless
billionaire Emilien de Montagne shatters her
sanctuary with a shocking proposition:
join his quest for revenge against the crown—
by becoming his royal wife!

Read Gisele and Emilien's story in

Princess Bride with Benefits

Available now!

And don't miss Claude's and Isabelle's stories,
coming soon!

PRINCESS BRIDE WITH BENEFITS

BELLA MASON

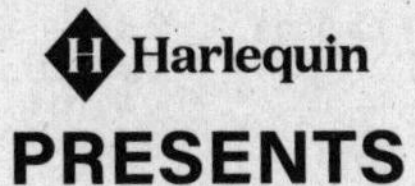

PRESENTS

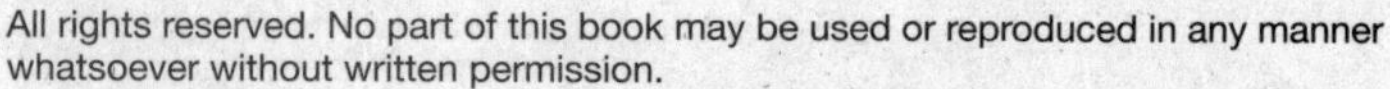

Recycling programs for this product may not exist in your area.

ISBN-13: 978-1-335-21395-2

Princess Bride with Benefits

Copyright © 2026 by Bella Mason

Harlequin Enterprises ULC
22 Adelaide St. West, 41st Floor
Toronto, Ontario M5H 4E3, Canada
www.Harlequin.com

HarperCollins Publishers
Macken House, 39/40 Mayor Street Upper,
Dublin 1, D01 C9W8, Ireland
www.HarperCollins.com

Printed in Lithuania

1 2 3 4 5 6 7 8 9 10 LIT 28 27 26 25

Bella Mason has been a bookworm from an early age. She has been regaling people with stories from the time she discovered she could hold the dinner table hostage with her reimagined fairy tales. After earning a degree in journalism, she rekindled her love of writing and she now writes full-time. When she isn't imagining dashing heroes and strong heroines, she can be found exploring Melbourne, with her nose in a book or lusting after fast cars.

Books by Bella Mason

Harlequin Presents

Awakened by the Wild Billionaire
Secretly Pregnant by the Tycoon
Their Diamond Ring Ruse
His Chosen Queen
Snowed-In Enemies

The De Luca Legacy

Strictly Forbidden Boss
Pregnant Before "I Do"

Visit the Author Profile page at Harlequin.com.

For my parents

For listening to the rambling stories of a four-year-old
and giving me my first taste of Greek mythology,
but if you read this book, let's never talk about it!

PROLOGUE

Ten years ago

GISELE SMOOTHED HER hands down her green dress, flattening it as she took a deep breath. Perhaps what she was wearing today would please her mother, but she wasn't holding out much hope. Gisele was a Princess of Alouette, an island Kingdom in the Mediterranean Sea off the coast of France, and as such her parents, the King and Queen, had very high expectations of her.

Unfortunately, the princess had always been found lacking. Gisele was eighteen but instead of living the life of a carefree teenager she had the weight of royal expectations sitting upon her shoulders. Not that she could wield any power, as the archaic laws of Alouette would never allow a woman to lead, so her older brother Claude—who was in the final year of study for his degree before commencing his military service next year—was destined for the throne.

Nor would Gisele have wanted that. What she so desperately wanted was freedom. Alas, that was never going to happen. Queen Agathe had very exacting expectations and Gisele would have to live up to them. Taking a deep breath, she placed her hand on the door handle, stepped out of her bedroom and headed down the long passages of the palace to the sun room where they would take their breakfast.

Gisele entered the bright room to find her family already sitting around a table laden with all sorts of food, a grand show of opulence that made her stomach turn. A photographer stood in the corner, snapping pictures. The clicking of the camera making Gisele's head hurt. The pictures were for yet another spread on the royal family: how close they were; how strong the familial bonds were. It was a farce, but image was everything.

Silently, Gisele took her seat and without missing a beat her mother's gaze shifted from the plate of fruit before her to appraise her daughter from head to toe. She frowned. Of course Gisele had been found wanting. She always was.

The queen exchanged a look with her husband at the head of the table and, as if by magic, a royal assistant appeared in the room and ushered the photographer away. Isabelle, who sat opposite Gisele, dropped her gaze to her food, refusing to look up. Claude sat beside her and had engaged their father in conversation, his arm on the table, fingers lazily hooked on the handle of his gold-rimmed coffee cup. From the snippets Gisele caught, she could tell it was about protesters of some sort; whatever her father was saying had caused the muscle in Claude's jaw to tick.

Gisele loved both her siblings with her whole heart, but she couldn't help but notice how much like her father Claude had become in recent years. Gone was the smile that he used to share with her when they'd grown up. In its place was only ever a frown, a sullen expression his constant companion these days. She knew that the loving boy was still inside her brother somewhere. The one who'd doted on her, even though he was only two years older, and had cuddled her and listened to her angst, but she feared she would never see him again.

'Gisele,' their mother began, 'Is that what you choose to wear to breakfast when you know how important this photo shoot was for our family? It's important to show how strong we are. Perfection is everything.' 'Strong' meaning untouchable, beyond reproach. But Gisele would never dare to correct her mother. 'You are the Princess of Alouette— you need to start acting like it.'

Her dress had been picked out by a stylist, her hair done by the best hairdresser in the palace, everything had been chosen to be perfect, and even so it was still not enough. 'Mother, can we not just have a civilised breakfast? Must we do this now?'

'Yes,' her mother bit out. 'You have to realise what you look like. You're taller than most princes, you haven't worked on your body, you refuse to do anything with your hair. How are we to show the world how polished and sophisticated the people of Alouette are when their princess won't even make an effort?'

Gisele noticed Claude pause his conversation and glance at her quickly before resuming speaking with her father. He wouldn't step in for her. Isabelle, at fourteen, could say nothing. And, if her mother's ire was focused on Gisele, then at least Isabelle would be spared. Still, Gisele wished she could be away from this place. Wished she could be anywhere but in this palace that was nothing but a gilded cage. Her jailers: the most powerful people in all the kingdom, her parents.

From the time she'd been young she had heard it all, everything that was ever wrong with her. The fact that she refused to colour her hair so that it would be as beautifully bronze as her mother's and Isabelle's, instead of being dull and boringly brown. How she was far too tall, taller even than her father. No one could ever want that in a wife, and she would need a powerful husband to satisfy her parents. How her body was nowhere near thin enough to squeeze into the designer dresses that a princess should wear.

She wished there was anyone to give her a kind word, but even her friends weren't really true friends. She had none of those. All she had was a social circle of acquaintances who were equally as cruel as her parents. A circle they had approved of because they were the ones who had chosen them. All she could do was count down the days until she would marry. At least then she would be away from here. And her departure would mean little to her parents, considering her total lack of power and influence.

Marriage was the only way she could have a life, the only way she would get any freedom at all. So, even though she was only eighteen, she prayed that someone would be willing to come to the palace and claim her hand. That she would be whisked to somewhere far away. That a powerful, handsome man would love her unconditionally and give her everything her heart craved, who would tell her she was perfect just the way she was.

Gisele, who had been about to reach for a dish of yoghurt—all she would have eaten under her mother's scrutiny—pulled her hand back, any appetite she might have had well and truly lost. And she had been hungry. She was often hungry, but she never dared eat her fill, not with her mother always watching her figure.

'I'm sorry I'm such a disappointment to you, Mother. Truly, I wish you could have had a daughter of whom you could have been proud.'

'Oh, stop being so dramatic, Gisele, and you *can* make

me proud. In fact, your father and I have been talking, and we know what you need to do.'

Part of Gisele wanted her parents to be proud of her, wanted to be the daughter that they desired, so she decided she would listen to what her mother had to say. Maybe whatever this was would make her life just a little bit easier so she wouldn't have to look in the mirror and see all the ways that she failed.

'What are you talking about, Mother?'

'We have arranged your marriage to Héctor Renaud, King of Valonova,' her mother said then took an elegant sip of coffee.

'What? You cannot be serious!' Gisele exploded, horrified. Even Claude had ceased speaking. 'He is old enough to be my father! What kind of man would even agree to marry me? I'm eighteen!'

'There you go being dramatic again. Can we cease with the histrionics, Gisele?' The almost bored way her mother spoke was a blade in Gisele's heart.

'Gisele,' her father called, 'You will listen to your mother.'

His voice brooked no argument, so Gisele quietened, swallowing every bit of horror and dread. Willing herself to keep the tears that burned behind her eyes at bay.

'You wouldn't actually marry until you were twenty-one, which gives us all enough time to introduce the idea of you and King Héctor as an item. We would make all the arrangements now, and little by little when the time came you would be perfectly accepted by the Kingdom of Valonova.'

'And would our kingdom accept him marrying their princess, who is so young? Do you realise he has a daughter who is a year younger than me? That his son is three years younger than me?'

'Our people *will* accept it. Our people will accept anything we tell them to and, once you are married, you will bear a child who would have Bettencourt and Renaud blood.'

That was all this was—a way to use her to obtain power in another kingdom. They kept showing her all the ways they didn't care about her as a daughter.

'So I'm just some sort of brood mare to you? One you can use to strengthen ties with other kingdoms? Have you no concern for me at all?'

'That is enough, Gisele! You are a princess. Your country comes before any sort of deluded ideas of romance. Is that what you're waiting for?' Queen Agathe scoffed. 'Don't be ridiculous. You should be thanking me. You would be married to a king, which is far more than you would ever attract on your own.'

'I can't do this.' Gisele felt as though she was on the verge of a panic attack. 'I can't do this any more.' She threw her napkin onto her plate and ran out of the room. When she reached the vibrantly flowering gardens, she was heaving deep breaths, dragging cool, ocean air into her lungs to try to clear the devastation from her mind, from her heart.

Marriage was supposed to be her freedom but, if she married King Héctor, she would be a prisoner in her own life for ever. She had to find a way out. There had to be a way to leave!

She rushed to her rooms, saying not a word to anyone she passed. The only thing she thought of was the sanctuary of her space and what she would do to escape. When she finally reached her bed chamber, she slammed the door behind her and sunk to the floor. Tears kissed her cheeks in a never-ending stream. And when she looked up at her opulent bedroom, seeing every piece of curated furniture and all the art hanging on the gilded wall—none of which she had chosen—a sob tore through her throat. Even this room was no sanctuary to her. Even this room was another place over which her parents had total control. She dragged herself off the floor and went listlessly to the bed.

Lying on the covers was her passport and a bank card. Under them lay a note. Astonished, Gisele picked it up.

All it said was: *Fly. Good luck.*

She didn't know who had given this gift to her, but someone was watching out for her. She would use their kindness and, under the cover of darkness she would leave that night. She would leave and she would find the life she had always wished for.

CHAPTER ONE

THE CLEAR-CELLOPHANE around the large bouquet of bright flowers crinkled in Emilien Montagne's hand as he climbed out of his sports car. A breath of cool ocean breeze kissed his skin as he took in the panoramic view of the Mediterranean Sea stretching towards the horizon in a carpet of vivid blue. It was a magnificent view for the villa he'd purchased for his mother, a stunning private residence in one of the most exclusive neighbourhoods of Sineaux, the capital city of the kingdom of Alouette.

He clutched the flowers tighter in his grasp as he walked up the stone path lined with lush green cypress trees to the large swivel door. A biometric pad beside the door handle lit up as he pressed his thumb against the reader, unlocking it, and in he stepped. The air was comfortably cool in here, as it always was, regardless of whether it was winter or summer. It was carefully monitored to constantly remain at the perfect temperature. The environment was always controlled, always ideal, for his ill mother to feel her very best.

The years hadn't been kind to Camille Montagne, Emilien's only parent. Cardiovascular disease had rendered her frail and the journey to diagnosis had not been an easy one. Emilien had been only a teenager when doctors had dismissed his mother's concerns as depression. Yes, she had been depressed after his father's passing, but it had only got worse and, as soon as Emilien was able to, he had found the best doctors in the world who had come back with the joint diagnoses of cardiovascular disease and depression. It was then that Emilien had decided his mother needed somewhere entirely stress-free to live, somewhere beautiful and calm. Somewhere he could provide the best round-the-clock care, somewhere where the doctors and carers answered to him.

Emilien walked through the house and out to the terrace, where he knew his mother would be basking in morning summer sunshine, admiring the view.

'Hello, Mama,' he said in greeting, with a smile he reserved only for her.

'Emilien!' Camille's face lit up as she moved to get off her lounger, but he stopped her from rising, instead taking a seat on the recliner next to hers.

'This is for you,' he said handing her the flowers. He noticed a bright-blue strap hung around her neck attached to a white square box that sat on her chest, peeking out of the neck of her low-cut blouse. The tiny screen displayed a steady heartbeat. He was used to seeing the holter monitor, but it was always an unpleasant reminder of how lucky he was to have every moment he did with her.

It was also a reminder of why he was here today. It was the anniversary of his father's death. For seventeen years, this had been the hardest day in the calendar. For seventeen years, Emilien had witnessed an extra-bright smile on his mother's face on this day to hide exactly how she was feeling.

'I wondered when you'd be coming.'

'I would have been here earlier, but I had to take care of some things first.' Being the CEO of Montagne Holdings left Emilien with very little personal time, but he loved it. He had taken Talaria Boats, a small boat manufacturer started by his grandfather, and turned it into an international powerhouse that not only built boats, but also luxury yachts. Then he had added on Sylph Motors, a luxury sports-car brand and, once that was going strong, he'd continued adding luxury brands to his stable by creating a real estate company, that had led him down the path of creating resorts. Thanks to Emilien's Midas touch, Montagne Holdings was a multi-billion-dollar company specialising in all that was luxurious.

'All that's important is that you are here now, *mon cœur*,' his mother said as she laid a warm hand on his cheek. 'Come, let's go put these in some water.' She picked up the bouquet of flowers, stood and moved into the house— much to Emilien's delight, for it was far too warm for her to be outside right now.

He watched his mother snip the ends off the flowers and arrange them in a vase. He would have done it himself, but he knew how much she hated it when he coddled her. So instead, he stood by and watched closely; any sign that this would be too much for her, and he would force her to rest.

'You know,' his mother said with a smile on her face, one that was both wistful and excruciatingly sad. 'Your father used to bring me flowers every Friday. Sometimes the old flowers wouldn't even be dead yet before I got new ones.'

'That's why there were always so many arrangements in the house,' Emilien added, feeling the stirrings of anger that he kept buried so deep for his mother's benefit.

His mother laughed softly. 'Yes. Sometimes I would press my favourite flowers in the bouquets between the pages of books. I still have them, you know—the flowers. Sometimes I'll open a book and find a rose pressed amongst the pages. Other times a daisy… It makes me feel like he's still with us.'

Emilien tried his hardest not to let his hands curl into the fists that he could feel forming at his sides. His heart was pounding in his chest. It had been nearly two decades and his mother's grief was still as raw now as it had been all those years ago. And he understood. What he wouldn't give to show his father what he had become, all that he achieved, what he had provided for his mother, but that wasn't possible because his father had been taken from them.

Seventeen years ago, Pierre Montagne had been an aristocrat and a prominent member of the Alouette parliament, one with a dream for a fair kingdom: one where people were taken care of and earned decent livings; where everyone could afford a comfortable life and good health care. Pierre had been murdered for that dream. His idealistic goal had been far too dangerous a prospect for the rich and arrogant, for the powerful, for the people who would benefit from having enough souls to step on.

He'd never have been allowed to get away with it. He had been found slumped over his office desk by his secretary, the tiniest of puncture holes in his neck. Nothing had ever been the same after that.

Emilien and his mother both knew exactly who was to blame for what happened: it was the royal family. Emilien had grown up with the knowledge that the king and queen had had his father killed. His mother had removed herself from society life entirely. She hadn't been able to be around the people she knew had had a hand in her husband's murder, or who weren't even upset that he had been killed. She'd withdrawn, and now lived a quiet life she had built for herself. She'd established a career of her own away from everybody else, but she'd never made friends again. She didn't trust anyone enough to do so.

Emilien had only been thirteen when his father had been killed; there was nothing he'd been able to do about it. Like Pierre Montagne before him, he was of noble blood, which entitled him to a seat in parliament once he was an adult, but after his father's death, he had given it up. Given up his father's dream. As a teenager hurt by Alouette's most powerful, he'd wanted nothing to do with ruling their country even if it meant severing any entitlement to that seat in the future. He was certain that he would never want it. But he wasn't a teenager any more. Now he was a thirty-year-old man with power that was far-reaching.

His mother was still fussing over her flowers but a tear ran down her cheek, lone and silent. He went to her and wiped it away.

'Mama,' he said gently, 'We go through this every year. At some point, you have to stop.'

'*Mon cœur*, when you love someone as your father and I loved each other, there will never be any stopping. Yes, this day is hard, but every day is hard. That pain never goes away.'

Emilien was aware of that. He had seen the hurt and vulnerability that loving someone so much, so purely, could cause. And that was why he vowed he would never put himself in the situation his mother was in. He would never let himself be so hurt, so destroyed, by the loss of another person.

His mother went to pick up the vase to place it on a nearby table but he took it from her hands. Putting it down, he made her look at him. 'I will make it right, Mama.'

Camille's eyes widened with alarm. 'What does that mean, Emilien?'

'I think you know,' he said

'No.' Panic was clear in her eyes. 'No! Those people are dangerous, Emilien. Please, I'm begging you, don't do anything.'

He took her hands in his, trying to reassure her. 'It will be fine, Mama. I know what I'm doing,' he said calmly.

'Promise me you won't. Promise me, Emilien. I can't lose my only child too. They'll never let you get away with anything, and then what will I do? I can't have lost my husband and my son!' Camille's voice rose higher and higher, becoming nearly hysterical. Emilien pulled her against his chest, hugging her small frame against his large one.

'Mama, calm down, please. Do you trust me?'

'Of course I do, you're my son.'

'Then trust that I know what I'm doing. I will be fine. Nothing will happen to me. I promise you, no one will take me away from you.'

'I can't lose you too.' His mother was crying, her tears forming a damp spot on his crisp white shirt.

'You never will, Mama. You never will.'

Turning his back on a life among the Alouette elite had made sense at the time. But it meant that now, when he wanted to cause the monarchy to implode, he needed to find a way back inside.

And he knew exactly how he'd do it.

CHAPTER TWO

Gisele Bettencourt stood behind the counter in a flower shop. Sunlight streamed in through the wide window front. By the far wall, flowers in jewel and pastel tones set in silver vases sat atop pillars of varying heights in a highly conceptual arrangement. A sprite made entirely of blossoms stood in the corner near the counter. A floral sentry watching over the shop. Buckets of bouquets created an aisle from the door into the store and led customers around the wide space full of baskets, vases and boxes.

Blooms were spread out on the countertop in front of Gisele, long stalks within her grasp. Meticulously, she added flower by flower to the bouquet in her hand, spinning it round and smiling as it grew in bright splashes of purples, blues and pinks, a little breath of white, some pops of green.

It always smelled so beautiful in here, as if she'd spread the attar of flowers in every nook and cranny of the space.

This was Gisele's happy place: Atelier Les Jardins. Her small flower shop in the town of Saint-Lorin-de-la-Mer. It was a beautiful little town near Marseilles, always packed with tourists and yachts in the Marina. Azure waters flowed all down the coast and stunning villas overlooked the sea. It was a quaint and lovely town attracting holidaymakers throughout the year. Billionaires had holiday homes here, and luxury hotels and resorts dotted the waterfront. There was glamour here, but there was also peace and tranquillity.

Gisele had settled in the town after having left Alouette ten years ago. She'd been only eighteen then, armed with a single bank card—with more money than she could have dreamed on it—her passport and a tiny suitcase filled with the bare essentials that she'd need to start a new life. She'd left the palace not knowing who was the saviour who had made her escape possible or where to go. Then she'd asked herself what she wanted and, after almost having been married to a man old enough to be her father, she realised she didn't want to be a princess. She just wanted to be an ordinary person living a peaceful life somewhere beautiful. So she bought a plane ticket to a place she always loved and moved to France.

Those early years weren't easy, but she had a great education and the determination to make something of her life, so she'd trained as a florist and opened this very shop. Now Atelier Les Jardins was the busiest florist in the town. Its reputation for creating breathtaking arrangements had spread far and wide, often attracting people from all over France.

Having a shop so renowned was the extent of the fame Gisele now had. She no longer appeared in papers and tabloids and magazines. There weren't any cameras hounding her wherever she went, no one told her what friends to make, what to wear, what to eat or how to behave. In the ten years since leaving the palace, she had found a quiet, ordinary life and she treasured it with her whole heart. She couldn't imagine giving this up for anything.

Gisele adored working with plants. She loved creating something beautiful that made people happy, something that could show someone that they were appreciated, or create a memory or tell them they were enough. Every flower was beautiful. It didn't matter how big they were, what colour they were or how their petals were shaped. Every unique flower just made an arrangement more interesting.

Best of all, flowers were honest. With them, there were no machinations she had to be aware of. Flowers didn't tear people down, they didn't plot or scheme and they weren't obsessed with power, they just existed. And that existence brightened the world.

But, as much as she loved her flowers, her little shop and her quiet life, she couldn't deny that she missed her siblings. Since leaving the palace, no one had been in contact with her. Her parents hadn't messaged her when they had found out she had left. Likely they would have seen it as some sort of betrayal, but she'd had to choose herself, because the life they'd been offering her was a prison sentence.

It had hurt to have evidence of how little she meant to them, that they hadn't seen her as a daughter. She had only ever been a princess to them, a piece on the chess board to be moved, with no will of her own. It hurt even more that she'd had no contact from either sibling in all that time. She'd known that was a risk when she'd left, but it was a risk she'd had to take.

Her youngest sister, Isabelle, would now be twenty-four and Gisele wondered what she was like. She wondered if Claude had found his way back to his old self or if he'd become even more like her father in the years she'd been gone. For now, the only means she had to know them was through social media, so she followed every page she could find that gave her any news of them, watching them grow via the anonymity of the internet, loving them from afar.

Gisele would've loved to find a way to keep in contact with her siblings, but she knew that wasn't possible. Either she would get sucked back into royal life or the choices she'd made would have consequences for Isabelle and Claude and she couldn't do that to either of them. So, for now, she had to be happy with this one-sided relationship through a phone screen.

Heaving a deep sigh, she wrapped brown paper around her finished bouquet and tied a bow made of raffia around the naked green stalks, before depositing it into one of the buckets hanging on the metal display stand by the door.

She tidied the counter and immediately got started on her next arrangement, another bright bundle of happiness. She was just about done putting in the last few roses when she spotted a gleaming black sports car drive up to the front of her store. Of course, such vehicles were a common sight in Saint-Lorin-de-la-Mer, so she paid little attention. It was likely yet another rich tourist. But, as the car parked in front of the window, she noticed the make: this particular model of Sylph sports car was rare anywhere in the world.

And then she saw the man in the driver's seat. The sun caught the bottom of his face; a harsh dark, diagonal shadow hid the top half. His illuminated jaw was covered in dark stubble. And what a jaw it was. Sharp and square, as if as if it had been carved straight out of marble. Lips that she could tell even from where she stood were pink and full. Lips she could imagine sinking her teeth into.

Gisele was transfixed. She no longer felt the rose in her grip. All she was aware of in that moment was the column of the mystery man's neck, thick and strong. And at the base of it a starched white collar curled around his throat, the button there undone, exposing the little dip that she could almost imagine placing her finger in. Caressing.

How smooth would that skin be? she wondered.

The man gracefully emerged from the car and buttoned up his charcoal-grey suit jacket, his hand flattening across the now connected quarters of the jacket that hid away most of the waistcoat beneath. Sunglasses were perched on his nose, a glimmer of light dancing off the metal frame, and she really wished she could see his eyes.

Abruptly, she realised that she had been staring at a stranger and averted her gaze, forcing herself to go back to her forgotten bouquet.

When was the last time anything distracted you from the flowers? She honestly couldn't remember. But, as she looked down at the flowers still scattered on the counter-top, she heard the bell above the door chime.

It was him. She knew it. He was in her store.

She couldn't explain how, but she could *feel* him walk to the counter, sucking the air from her lungs with every step. In her periphery she spied him pull off his sunglasses in a smooth motion, letting them dangle from the tips of his long, elegant fingers that made her own twitch.

'Maybe you should let go of that,' a voice said to her, so deep it could have been made out of gravel. It was laced with amusement, a hint of flirtation.

Gisele looked up. Stunning hazel eyes, a marble of brown and green, stared back at her. There was an intensity to them. It was as if they were black holes pulling all her focus into them. And the man was tall, taller than she had realised.

It was exceptionally rare that anyone made her feel small, but he did. He must have been nearly two metres tall. If she pressed her body to his, her head would fit comfortably under his chin. How wonderful would that embrace be?

Everything about this man was perfect, from his dark-brown, perfectly cut hair to his impeccably tailored suit.

There was not a strand out of place. It was as if even dust had deemed him too powerful to sully. And, when Gisele looked at what had his attention, she noticed a crimson drop dangling at the edge of her palm. The rose she had been working with was still clutched in her hand and a thorn had pricked her sufficiently to draw blood. She hadn't felt it.

Heat rushed to her cheeks as she quickly grabbed a bit of paper towel and dabbed away the evidence of her transfixion. 'Sorry about that,' she apologised. What kind of impression must she have given this man who she was certain had travelled a distance to her come to her store? He certainly wasn't local. She would have remembered him, and the way her stomach was currently somersaulting. Instead of assisting him, she was picturing what his embrace would be like! How could he cloud her mind like that just by stepping into her shop? 'Can I help you?'

She noticed his pupils flare as she spoke, then he cleared his throat, lightening the gravel just a touch. 'I'm certain you're the only one who can.'

The way he looked at her made the shop shrink in size. The air became thicker, but his words made her certain that he had come due to Atelier Les Jardins' renown.

'What's the occasion, and what sort of arrangement are you looking for?' She reached beneath the counter and pulled out a notepad and pen so she could write down as many notes as possible about his order.

'The event is a wedding, and the arrangement is a mutually beneficial one.' He placed his right hand on the counter so close to hers that Gisele thought he might touch her, but the slight movement of his arm told her that, at the last moment, he'd chosen not to. Instead, he leaned against the countertop, bringing their faces a smidge closer, his grey coat spreading open a little.

Gisele's brows knit in confusion. That wasn't the kind of answer customers usually gave. Butterflies were frantically fluttering in her stomach, and something about his words made the hairs on the back of her neck stand up. 'Who are you?'

'My name is Emilien René Montagne, and I know that you are Princess Gisele Elise Bettencourt.'

Gisele felt the blood drain from her face, and she began to back away. 'My parents sent you,' she breathed in terror, as he stepped round the counter. 'Y-you're not allowed b-back here,' she stammered.

Her assistant was at the back of the shop. All Gisele would need to do would be to scream and they would come running—but what then? Was this Emilien as ruthless as her parents? Would she be putting her assistant in harm's way? The word, 'Help…' died on her tongue before it ever had a chance to fly.

'Your parents have done no such thing and, even if they had sent someone, I would be the last person they would choose.'

This man wasn't crowding her. Even though he had forced his way back here, he wasn't intimidating her in all the ways she would have expected. His voice was calm, he didn't try to grab her, but still something didn't sit right. And, even though he kept a small space between them, he was taking up all her capacity to think, but she needed to try.

'Montagne,' she said quietly. The name stirred something in the recesses of her memory. 'I don't know what you want, Mr Montagne, but I think you should leave.' It was a miracle she managed to say anything through her parched mouth, but she was proud of the fact that she managed to tell him that she needed him to go. Even if, inexplicably, a crazy part of her wanted him to stay.

'I need to talk with you,' he said. She saw his hand flex towards her then curl at his side. He let out a sigh and took a minute step back. Suddenly she could breathe again. 'This is urgent, Gisele. Is there somewhere private we could speak?'

Gisele's heart was hammering in her chest. She couldn't remember a time she'd been so afraid. Well, maybe that was a lie. She remembered how terrified she'd been before she'd left the palace. She couldn't go back. She couldn't listen to whatever this man had to say.

'I'm not going anywhere with you.' It was the smartest choice, when he must have ties to her parents and had affected her sensibilities from the moment he'd driven his car up to the store.

She could see his frustration in the press of his lips. 'I have nothing to do with the royal family. What I do have is a matter of grave importance. A sensitive matter. So it would be best if we spoke in private.' He ran an aggravated hand through his hair, mussing the perfect style. Somehow, it didn't take away from his immaculate image; it almost made him look better, as if there was something wild beneath those still, calm waters. That the glossy surface was a deception.

'Look,' he said, 'I will be in town for a few days. Here's my card.' He placed a perfect white rectangle on the counter, not even attempting to hand it to her. On it, embossed in sharp silver lettering, was his name, and below that it read: *CEO, Montagne Holdings.* 'There's a restaurant by the pier. Meet me tonight at eight. I will answer any of your questions and then you will have to listen to what I need to say.'

Gisele didn't respond, but whatever Emilien Montagne saw on her face made him sigh once again and he turned on his heel to leave the shop.

Frozen, Gisele watched him stride towards the door. On the threshold, he paused and looked back at her over his shoulder, something simmering in his gaze before he exited and made for his car.

She watched him drive away before she picked up the card and tucked it away in her pocket, certain that she would never call the number on it. She'd had worked far too hard to obtain this peaceful life.

'I'm staying far away from you, Emilien Montagne.'

CHAPTER THREE

EMILIEN AGGRESSIVELY BROUGHT his car to a stop in front of a quaint villa. Annoyance drummed a pounding rhythm in his body. He hadn't been able to shake his irritation all night. Only one thing would: talking to Gisele. And that was the reason he had come here—to Gisele's home.

The walls looked old. The accents around it were blue, to match the sea that was only a few paces away. Pots of different sizes with different shapes and colours of flowers lined the stone steps and led to a small garden that was so vibrantly bright. It was such a cheerful space. He couldn't imagine having something like that in his life.

He had waited the night before, at the restaurant by the pier, just as he'd said he would. He had chosen a table from which the water outside could be seen, a black mirror which had breathed in a gentle rise and fall as it reflected the gold and silver lights of the restaurant and boats nearby.

He had picked the restaurant in the hope that a dinner somewhere public but discreet would ease the princess's nerves enough to meet him, to talk to him. Even the table had been chosen so that she would know that she could be seen from the outside: assurance that he wouldn't try to harm her, that there would be witnesses if he did. Those weren't considerations he usually offered when he negotiated with people. Normally those entering into a deal with him knew that Emilien had the most power at the table.

And what had Gisele done with his generosity? In a staggering show of effrontery, she hadn't shown up. He had been stood up. No one had ever done that to Emilien before. No one had dared to! The audacity was mind-blowing, but it was proof that, while she wasn't living as one, Gisele was a royal through and through. Either that or she was genuinely terrified of him. Neither option worked for him, which had him looking through her fact file for her address.

Emilien killed the engine and stepped out of the car, leaning against the side of it. Gisele could try to hide from him, but he needed to talk to her, and now there would be no getting away from him.

The sun was still very low in the sky. It was too early for most people to head to work just yet, especially in a town such as this. But, given that Gisele was a florist, he was fairly certain that she would have to head out early, so he just had to be earlier. Emilien could be patient when he wanted to be. He'd wait.

But he didn't have to wait all that long before Gisele appeared. Today she wore a flowing skirt and bright top. It did nothing to quell the attraction he felt for her. It possibly only made it worse.

The encounter with Gisele at her shop had frustrated him. He'd known exactly what Princess Gisele looked like. He had an entire fact file on her sitting in an encrypted folder on his personal server. The knowledge had done absolutely nothing to prepare him for the onslaught of her presence the moment he had walked into that florist. He had been drawn to her. She possessed a beauty so rare, he was certain no human could have birthed her. Certainly, she was placed on earth by some higher being.

He'd known the facts about her, like her exact height in centimetres: one hundred and eighty five. Her hair and eye colour: brown. Her schooling: a combination of home schooling and École Artois. Training: BP Fleuriste from the European School of Florists in Marseilles. But that had made no difference when he'd seen her.

He'd seen that her height made her so perfect to stand by his side. Emilien was certain she hadn't met many men who could make her feel safe and protected, but he could. His body could form a shield around hers and he'd still be able to place a kiss on the top of her head.

In pictures, her hair had always been perfectly coiffed but there, at the shop, her brown locks, so glossy, had just been pulled back from her face, presumably to make it easier to work. The simple style had also taken away any distraction from a face so perfect, he could have wept. It was almost cherubic. And, as she had continued working with the flowers before her, her teeth pressed into a bottom lip so full, so pink, that all he could think about was kissing her. Something about her had drawn him forward in a magnetised way. And, when he had reached the counter, he'd noticed that she wasn't arranging that bouquet at all. She'd been grasping a rose in her hand so tightly that it had drawn blood. And he'd wanted to pull that rose away and toss it in the dirt for having dared to harm such a stunning creature.

But he hadn't done that because he had control. Instead, he had challenged her in what he had hoped was as charming a way as possible and had asked her if perhaps she should let go of the rose. That was when she had looked up at him. The effect of those eyes had been a punch to the gut.

Emilien was familiar with the entire royal family, but Gisele was somehow set apart from them by the universe. Where they all had green eyes, hers were the warmest brown. The gold in them had beckoned him like the warmth of the sun after it had been chilly for too long. And, when he had gone behind the counter and seen the entirety of her, his fingers had ached to touch her even though she'd been clad in something as ordinary as jeans and a T-shirt. He hadn't been able to help but notice her hourglass figure, those soft round curves so much fuller than he would have expected on a princess of Alouette, but so beautiful.

And, given all that he needed to achieve to right the wrongs done to his family, the attraction that he clearly had towards her was very, *very* unwelcome.

Then there was the way she'd reacted to him—the fear in her eyes when she'd thought her parents had sent him. He knew something must have happened for her to disappear but seeing that fear had enraged him. He wanted to know exactly what had happened.

There was no way she'd have spoken to him at Atelier Les Jardins when she had looked like a deer in the headlights. She'd clearly wanted to run as far away from him as she could. Every step forward he had taken meant she had taken one back, as if he was some sort of predator stalking his prey. And yes, maybe to some degree he was, but not in a way that she should fear. The only people who should fear him were the King and Queen of Alouette. Which was exactly why he was going to ignore the attraction to her. There were more important things at stake.

And it was also the reason he was keeping his temper in check this morning, despite his annoyance.

Gisele finally descended the few stone steps, her expression morphing from one that was neutral, if a little melancholy, to one that was apprehensive but clearly very angry. That was fine. Anger, Emilien could deal with. Anger, he knew. Anger had long been his friend.

'What are you doing here?' she asked frostily.

'I've already told you I have an urgent matter to discuss with you which I will not be doing on the street.' Emilien had to remain calm. He didn't move from where he was, back pressed against the body of his car.

Gisele crossed her arms over her chest. 'I'm not going anywhere with you, Mr Montagne. I thought I made that perfectly clear yesterday.'

'And I made it clear that we had an urgent matter to discuss, princess.' The title made her eyes widen in alarm, having the effect he wanted. A subtle reminder that he knew exactly who she was. 'Now, we can talk inside, we can speak in my car or we can find somewhere else. It's your choice.' And that was all the choice he was going to give her.

'I don't know you and I don't trust you. I'm not letting you into my home and I'm not getting into your car. Like I said, I'm not going anywhere with you.'

Emilien finally pushed off the car and, with sure steps, moved to stand before Gisele. She was close enough to touch, not that he would. 'You don't have to trust me for us to talk. And, just so you know, it's very rude to stand someone up when they invite you to dinner.'

Gisele huffed a breath so full of exasperation that it nearly made him laugh.

'You're not going away, are you?' she said, looking completely unimpressed.

'No.'

She turned away, looking down the street, probably hoping for some sort of salvation to save her from him, but none would come. Nothing would dare challenge Emilien Montagne. He knew who he was.

When Gisele turned back to look at him, he noticed her

eyes rove over his body from the top of his head down to his toes and all the way back to his eyes. Interesting... Now this he could work with.

Emilien plastered a lazy smile on his face. He had to admit, it was far easier than he might have expected to turn on the charm for her. Probably because he still so desperately wanted to kiss her. He wanted to touch that perfect porcelain skin—so odd, when her family looked so different.

'Look, Gisele, I understand that you don't want to speak to me. I get it. I've turned up out of nowhere, you don't know me, but would I have come all this way to speak to you if there wasn't a situation that truly warranted it? You must know who I am. My time is precious, so surely you could have dinner with me? I hear the seafood here is excellent. So maybe we could have a friendly chat somewhere you're comfortable, over a glass of Sancerre. How does that sound to you?'

'I must be completely out of my mind,' he heard her mumble. But then she straightened up and looked him in the eye. Beyond the trepidation and fear, there was fire in Gisele. A hidden strength that he wouldn't underestimate. 'Fine. Mr Montagne—'

'It's Emilien,' he interrupted.

'You're not a friend of mine; it's Mr Montagne.' She reached into her handbag. The movement brought his attention to the way the strap lay across her body, emphasising the fullness of her breasts, and he needed to close his eyes to get his body under control. When had a woman last affected him like this?

Gisele quickly scribbled out a note, tore it out of her notepad and handed it to him. 'Here. You can meet me at seven tonight. Don't be late.'

She turned round and walked into her house without a

backward glance, and he was once again reminded that, even though Gisele Bettencourt might be hiding in Saint-Lorin-de-la-Mer, she was, in fact, still a princess.

CHAPTER FOUR

GISELE WALKED ALONG a bright path surrounded by green plants and shrubbery, lush trees and bright flowers. Despite it being nearly seven p.m., the summer sun was still high in the sky, and there were plenty of people strolling about the elaborate gardens in Saint-Lorin-de-la-Mer. The path that she was on led to a restaurant at the far end of the gardens—a restaurant that belonged to a good friend of hers, and the name of which she had given to Emilien as the place that they would meet.

She came here often and knew the chef well. He was one of her most loyal customers, ordering their every arrangement from her. Gisele didn't trust Emilien, but she did trust her friend and the waiters in his establishment, so when Emilien had demanded that they find somewhere to speak this was the first place she'd thought of.

She followed the paths of spectacular flowers, bisecting swirling quadrants to a building made of stone. Dark, arched windows made it look almost fortress-like, ancient, even though she knew it wasn't. When she entered, it was as if all the bright light outside had been drawn into a void where it was cast into nothing. Deep-grey stone walls met black tables and a charcoal carpet underfoot. The walls were illuminated in raining beams of red light. The effect gave the feeling of being in the catacombs under Paris, a complete juxtaposition to the scene just outside the restaurant walls. But it wasn't dreary, nor was it frightening; it couldn't be, not with the myriad flowers arranged around the space, picked out be strategically placed under gold-hued lights.

Floral arrangements led her to the *maître-d'* who, in turn, led her towards the back of the restaurant. The flowers grew increasingly more sparse the closer she went towards the private dining room, as if to say that from that point there would be no distractions. Not even a floral arrangement would disturb whatever happened behind those walls, which was appropriate, because she was sure whatever Emilien had to say should not be heard by anyone but her.

Just like the main area of the restaurant, the private dining room was dimly lit in gold and red light. A black smoked-glass partition separated her from the rest of the patrons. It still allowed her a view of the entrance across the dining space, but she knew that, from the outside, no one would be able to see through the smoked-mirrored surface. The thought might have been concerning if she had been somewhere unfamiliar, but here all she would have to do was shout and any number of people would come running. So, even though she was isolated from everyone else, she felt safe.

Or, safe enough. She suspected that Emilien was one of those powerful men that no one could really stop. He was beyond being controlled, which meant she had to take every precaution of her own.

One of those precautions was arriving earlier than him.

Once she had taken her seat, the *maître-d'* gave her a reassuring smile and left the room. Gisele took a deep breath. She'd intended to steady her nerves but she looked through that glass panel and saw Emilien enter the restaurant. A breath was no solution when his presence even this far away affected her heartbeat so violently.

He looked towards the private dining room and, even though she knew he couldn't see her, she felt that gaze burn right into her. She felt it like a scalding touch on her body. Felt it in the tingling of her fingers and clenching in her stomach. She had to brace herself for anything he could say, but she also had to brace herself for the man himself. This man who might want to take her back to Sineaux. If he did want that, he had another thing coming.

She watched Emilien walk through the restaurant towards her, her heartbeat rapidly increasing with his every step. He was a threat to her she was resolved to keep her distance from, and yet her body did not get the memo. This attraction to him didn't feel like a brief appreciation, it felt like something that was built into every cell in her body.

Then he was opening the door. Stepping inside. Shrinking the lavish dining room so it suddenly felt ten times smaller. The air ten times thinner. The polite thing to do would be to stand and greet him, but there was no way she'd be able to do that, so she remained seated and watched him sit opposite her.

'Princess,' he greeted her with a playful smirk, yet the look in his eyes was far from light-hearted. There was a dark intensity to them. Green and brown glittered with the light dancing in them like tiny stars. It really was unfair how beautiful he was, but she couldn't get caught up in that. He was a wolf and she was prey.

'Mr Montagne,' she replied.

He sat down and undid his napkin with a flick, casually draping it over his lap. 'I see we're still not on a first-name basis.'

'And it will remain that way if I can help it.'

He rested his arms on the curved arm rests of the black, cushioned chair. 'We'll see, princess.'

She hated that he kept calling her that. She didn't need a reminder of the life she'd left. But, before she could say anything to put an end to the taunt his use of her title clearly was, the door opened and in walked waiters who carried in and placed plates of seafood before each of them, beautiful artworks in shades of white and green, a delectable foam creating a sea within the plate that made the seafood appear as little islands. Their glasses were filled with a chilled white wine that was then placed in a silver bucket that stood beside the table.

Once they had everything they needed, one of the waiters turned to her and said, 'If you require anything else, madam, simply call for us.'

She knew exactly what he meant and gave him a grateful smile. It dropped off her face as soon as she was alone with Emilien.

'You wanted seafood and Sancerre? Well, here it is.'

'You ordered for me.' Disbelief coloured his tone. She was sure no one else would have had the audacity, but she had a life to protect, so she had indeed ordered the meals when she had called to make the reservation.

'The sooner we eat, Mr Montagne, the sooner this dinner will be over, allowing us to leave and never come back. So I suggest you stop wasting time and talk.'

The asshole laughed.

'I can tell you're hiding your nerves with this bravado, but you don't have to be nervous. I really am not here to deliver you back to your family—quite the opposite, in fact.

So how about we take a small breath and start over?' He held his hand out to her over the table. 'My name is Emilien Montagne, but you can call me Emilien. What's yours?'

'This is ridiculous,' Gisele groused, but he was right. She was trying to hide her nervousness with antagonism, and that wasn't who she usually was, so grudgingly she reached for his hand.

The instant she shook it, she gasped. The heat of the touch travelled throughout her body, taking her breath and settling in her stomach.

'I'm Gisele,' she said a tad breathlessly, and pulled her hand away as quickly as possible, hoping that he didn't notice, but when she looked at him his eyes had darkened just a smidge. 'So what is the opposite of delivering me to my family? Are you looking to move to Saint-Lorin-de-la-Mer, Emilien? I find that hard to believe.' She placed her hands on her lap beneath the table, her skin still aflame.

He leaned forward, elbows on the dark table cloth, and said, 'And you would be right. I am not looking to do that. What I come with is an offer of protection from your family that will allow you to live the life you want, *if* you form an alliance with me.'

'I already have the life I want, and it's obvious you need my help, because why else would you be here? If it was really about me, you would have come years ago, but it's not. What I don't know is how I could possibly help you.'

Emilien sat back in his chair and brought his wine glass to his lips studying her as he took a long sip of the crisp French wine. He placed the glass back down with lazy ease and picked up his utensils. Not wanting to give him the satisfaction of knowing he was getting to her, Gisele did the same.

'Are you really happy, though?' he asked, bringing a

morsel of the artistically displayed food to his mouth, chewing politely. When he swallowed, Gisele couldn't tear her eyes from his throat.

What is happening to me? She wasn't completely inexperienced. She had been with men before, but she'd never felt like this. 'I think I'd know if I was happy or not, Emilien.'

'Really? Are you sure about that? Do you not miss your brother and sister? Don't you want contact with them?'

Of course she wanted contact with them. She missed her siblings so much that it felt like a piece of her heart was constantly missing, a piece that she'd never find. And her parents were to blame for that. They'd committed many crimes against her for which they would never face any repercussions and how she wished there was a way for her to get back at them in some way. But it was impossible.

'You can't promise me that, and to taunt me with it is cruel,' she said softly, pushing her food around her plate.

'I know what it's like to lose family because of your parents, Gisele. And what I'm looking for is simply the power that can't be your own to possess.'

Gisele dropped her folk with a clatter. Finally, realisation had dawned: she knew *exactly* what Emilien was after. Thanks to the archaic patriarchal laws of Alouette, that neither her grandfather nor her father had ever sought to change because it had always served them, princesses could hold no political power.

But their spouses could. Being a princess of Alouette would mean strengthening ties to other countries when she married. It meant attracting the right sort of power into the monarchy, a means to have the right men ruling the country. She hated it with every fibre of her being.

'You're out of your mind.' Her chair scraped loudly against the floor as she stood. She bunched her napkin in her hand as she threw it on the table. She'd heard enough. She was leaving right now. But a hand shot out and grabbed her arm, the touch branding her. An electric current took her breath away, born of the meeting point where his skin met hers, and she was certain that there would be a permanent mark there, forever reminding her of this moment and of this man.

She looked back, startled, and saw Emilien swallow hard. The flame of desire flashed brightly on his face too. She snatched her hand away and he let go as if he had been burnt.

'You're no different to everyone else in the life I escaped,' she managed, her voice a near whisper. 'Everyone has always wanted to use me.'

Emilien looked up at her from his seat. When he spoke, his voice had dropped a register. 'I only want to right a wrong, Gisele. That's all I want. And, given that you ran away from royal life to settle here, I can only imagine that you were wronged too. I can give you a chance to rewrite your story.'

'You can't promise that,' she said, shaking her head, emotion clogging her throat.

'Wouldn't you like to speak to your siblings again?'

'Of course I would, I would give anything for that chance, but I know it's not possible.'

'I understand that feeling but, unlike you, I will actually never get the chance because of what your parents did.'

'What did my parents do?'

A look of utter anguish passed over his face before he managed to hide it away. She desperately needed to know.

'Tell me.'

'They murdered my father.'

Gisele sank back into her chair, unsure as to what to say.

What could she say to that? All the fight left her body. How could she be angry at this man for seeking her out when, if the roles had been reversed and she had come from a loving family, she might have looked for any way to find justice for them too? But her parents were the King and Queen. No one in Alouette could possibly take them on. No one would win against the crown.

Emilien looked relaxed in his chair but his grip on the arm rests betrayed his emotion. 'Have you ever heard of my father? His name was Pierre Montagne.'

The name rang a bell, and she was taken back to a time when she'd been only a child wandering the halls of the palace, hearing stories. Some of it she'd understood, some she hadn't.

'I remember the name,' she said. 'I was eleven at the time.' A child in training to be a princess. Training that had not included politics, but she did remember the media coverage, and she did remember that her parents had seemed completely unbothered by it all. But so little had ever bothered them.

'My father,' Emilien said, pushing his plate away and placing his arms on the dining table, 'Was trying to make a difference in Alouette. He was negotiating between parliament, the corporations and unions for better wages and benefits—things that made him unpopular with the royals and the upper echelons of the kingdom.'

'But it also made him popular with the people,' Gisele guessed.

'Exactly.' Emilien drew abstract shapes on the table cloth, clearly remembering things from a long time ago, repeating a story that had settled within him over time. How many times had he told this story? she wondered.

'The people questioned the usefulness of the monarchy and there were protests to overthrow your parents,' he continued.

'I remember that—the protests. When I left ten years ago, there were still people who were unhappy, and that didn't sit well with my parents.' She still remembered Claude and her father talking about it during that last breakfast. Thinking about Claude made her heart hurt.

'No, it wouldn't.' Emilien's gaze lifted to meet hers and she was unable to look away. 'Those protests resulted in my father's assassination.'

'I'm so sorry, Emilien. I know words alone can't ever make this right, but I fail to see how I fit into all of this.'

'I intend to take up my father's cause.'

'And that would require a seat in parliament.'

He nodded.

Gisele could understand that. It seemed he'd loved his father, so it would make sense that he'd want to honour his memory. But she was also no fool. She knew a man like Emilien couldn't possibly just want to see his father's cause brought to fruition—he would want justice, revenge. There was more to this plan that he wasn't telling her, and the very thought of it made Gisele nervous.

But the intensity in Emilien's gaze, his posture, made it plain how much this meant to him. And there was a part of her that understood his need for revenge, because that part of her wanted some sort of retribution against her parents for her own treatment. She'd just never seen a way to get that, not without hurting Claude and Isabelle. And that was assuming she had any chance of success, which she didn't, because her parents held too much power. It didn't matter that Gisele was their daughter; they would do away with her without a single regret if she challenged them.

That was why she fully believed Emilien's story: she

already knew what her parents were capable of. But, no matter how much she wanted to help him, she couldn't do so at the expense of herself.

'You still haven't said the words,' she said at last. 'You haven't said exactly what you want, and if you want my help you need to be forthright. I've had enough of manipulative people. I can't trust that.'

She watched him study her, uncomfortable with how much those hazel eyes might see, because it felt as if he saw right through her.

'I need you to marry me to give me that seat in parliament. I understand it might seem drastic, but we only really need to be married for a year.'

'Because we need to be married for a minimum of a year and living together in all that time for you to keep that seat.'

'Yes,' he replied. 'And in return I will give you anything you want.'

Gisele laughed and it sounded sad even to herself. She took a sip of wine and glanced around at their dimly lit surroundings.

'What is it?'

She placed her glass back on the table and played with the stem. 'I always hoped that marriage would give me freedom, a life free of my parents, one that could maybe make me happy. This just doesn't feel like what I had imagined.' She looked up to find him watching her. 'Can you really give me freedom and my siblings back without retaliation from my parents? That feels a little fantastical.'

He reached across the table and placed his large hand on hers, stilling it from troubling the wine glass. 'If you understand that happiness does not mean love, I can give you that, princess. I'm a powerful man; there's nothing that I couldn't give you. We could have a successful alliance, and you'd get the life you always wanted. I give you my word.'

'The word of a stranger means little.' Gisele looked away from him. He made things sound so simple, but they weren't. She had set down roots that couldn't be easily removed. 'I can't just up and leave with you. I have a life here, a business. There are people who rely on me for their livelihoods. I want to help you, Emilien, but it's just not possible.'

'I fully appreciate the sacrifice I am asking you to make, but I'm not asking you to give up your business or your life. I would make it possible for you to run things from wherever you are.'

Gisele laughed. 'That may be possible for you, but not even you can make flower arrangements virtually. You're asking me to give up something I love for a whole year. Would you stop running Montagne Holdings for a year if the roles were reversed?'

'No,' he replied.

'Thought so. You can't expect that of me, then.'

'My answer is no because I have already structured my business in a way that I can run it from anywhere in the world.'

'Says the man who doesn't have to assemble the cars himself.'

'Yes, our businesses may be different, but I am only asking you to give up the things that require your physical presence.'

'The parts that bring me peace, you mean.'

'Look, I will help you in any way you need during this year. I will make it possible for you to run a successful shop and, while we are together, I will be at your disposal and help you grow Atelier Les Jardins. I can teach you things about business that no classroom can. That many other entrepreneurs don't know. I'm willing to meet you halfway and, in return, I just require your help.'

She understood what he needed and why he had come to her, but she just couldn't give him the yes he was looking for. Not without carefully considering every aspect of his request.

At this point she was leaning towards no.

'I need to think about it.'

CHAPTER FIVE

GISELE'S SHOES BEAT a steady rhythm on the wooden slats of the marina pathway. The afternoon sun glinted on the water's surface like tiny, embedded diamonds rising and falling with the current. There were hundreds of boats in the marina, most of them white, but all of them with different pops of colour. Some with sails, some without. It wasn't often that she came out here. She'd never really had a reason to, until today.

Atelier Les Jardins supplied so many local businesses with floral arrangements that she had created quite a network for herself, and it was precisely through this network that she had discovered that Emilien was not staying at any of the resorts or hotels in Saint-Lorin-de-la-Mer, but on a boat.

All she knew about the vessel itself was that it was called *Empyrean Drift*. Gisele couldn't imagine why Emilien would choose to stay on a boat when, in a town that functioned as a playground for so many billionaires, there were so many luxurious amenities on land.

She kept walking until she saw the name on a stern. And it was suddenly obvious to her exactly why he'd chosen to stay here instead of any hotel. This was no mere boat. *Empyrean Drift* was a mega yacht, clearly the biggest in the marina and furthest away from all the other vessels. It was so big, in fact, that from where Gisele stood she couldn't possibly take it all in. Why would Emilien need to check in to a hotel when he had a floating one all to himself?

She was a princess, and therefore no stranger to displays of wealth, but this was on another level. She had been out on her parents' boat before, but compared to this that seemed less like a yacht and more like a skiff.

While most of the other yachts and boats were white, this was different. The hull was a deep, almost navy-blue colour. She could imagine how that would render it virtually invisible on the open sea. And the tall storeys above it were white with gleaming silver railings and sparkling windows. It was quite literally a jewel sitting on the water.

Gisele steeled herself and walked up the gangway. She had to talk to Emilien. There was no hiding from him. If she didn't go to him, he would come to her. At least this way she would be the one making a move and no one would do it for her.

She had been thinking about his proposal all day. She had barely slept the night before after their dinner. She had given up on sleep altogether long before the sun came up but, no matter how much she thought about it, she still didn't have an answer for Emilien's proposition. She kept wavering between helping him and steering clear of him, but there was no denying the responsibility she felt towards him, towards helping him, because, after all, it was *her* family who had hurt his. That was why she had ignored the impulse within her to refuse his proposition outright.

Someone must have told him that she'd arrived because she hadn't even got to the top of the gangway when she saw Emilien waiting for her. And then she had to recognise that it wasn't just wanting to help him that had her considering saying yes. She couldn't deny that she was drawn to him. It was as if they were meant to know each other, which was completely ludicrous, because she didn't want to know anyone who had any dealings with the power players of Alouette. And yet her steps quickened. Her heart beat furiously in her chest and her soul tried to reach out for his. How would she ever steer clear of that?

'Good evening, princess,' Emilien said, holding out his hand. She knew exactly what that touch would feel like and still she put her hand in his. This time she didn't gasp at the current that travelled between them, she just let it wash over her. It was impossible to fight a wave and so much easier to let the water crash over you.

'I'm assuming you have an answer for me.'

'I might,' she said as she stepped aboard.

'Come, let's go to the deck where we can talk.'

Which one? she almost asked, but she didn't. She simply followed.

He took her up to the sun deck and she was glad at that choice. It was high up here. She could see the other decks below her, but she could also see so much of the marina and the beaches nearby. It gave her a whole new appreciation of Saint-Lorin-de-La-Mer.

'Make yourself comfortable. I'll get us some drinks.'

She watched Emilien disappear through a set of open glass doors, the panels stacked to each side, and walk out to the rail.

What should I do?

Hoping to force her mind towards a decision, she pulled out her phone and opened her social media apps. She didn't spare a look for any notifications on any of her own posts— she hardly made any and the few she did make were to do with her flowers. Instead, she typed her brother's and sister's names into the search engine and waited just a second until it loaded posts about Claude and Isabelle. Just wanting to catch a glimpse of them, she picked one at random—a post that was a day old, which showed her sister's smiling face.

Isabelle had always been beautiful, but that beauty had only grown with her. Gisele's stomach roiled with guilt as it always did when she looked at pictures of Isabelle—guilt at having left her little sister to the wolves of the palace. What kind of life did she have? When Gisele had lived there, Isabelle had only been fourteen, and their mother's scrutiny had been focused on Gisele. But with Gisele out of the picture that scrutiny would have needed another target, and she was certain it must have landed on her little sister.

Whatever Isabelle had gone through since then was undoubtedly Gisele's fault. So while she might feel a responsibility to help Emilien, she absolutely felt a responsibility to help Isabelle.

But was she brave enough to do that?

Emilien returned with two glasses on a tray. He'd asked his chef for something refreshing and non-alcoholic. He and Gisele had a lot to discuss, important matters that needed a clear head and absolute consent.

His chef had offered to have someone bring it out to him, but Emilien had refused and insisted that he should be given complete privacy. His staff was discreet, and he trusted them implicitly, but he never trusted anyone enough to allow them information that they could trade, and for his scheme to work he needed the royal family to be in the dark until he revealed his plans.

When he entered the deck area, Gisele painted a lonely picture at the back of his boat, head bent, a crease between her eyebrows, her lips turned down at the corners. He placed the tray down on a table between two loungers and carried the drinks in his hand. Silently, he walked up behind her and looked over her shoulder at the phone screen holding her attention.

Isabelle, the younger princess of Alouette, looked back at him.

It was clear that Gisele missed her siblings. Emilien could only imagine just how much not being able to see them must hurt her, but he still couldn't stop the fury that built in him at the thought. Her family was alive—she *could* see them, reunite with them. His father was dead. Still, instead of growing angry at her, he tried to offer her comfort.

'Your sister runs a children's charity,' he said, startling Gisele. She looked from her phone to his eyes and he could see in hers the emotion she was trying so hard to keep at bay. 'She's the perfect princess. The people love her. Your parents might not always be popular, but I think everyone loves Isabelle.'

'You don't know what it means to hear someone who lives there say that.' She turned away quickly but he still caught the glassy sheen in her eyes.

What he didn't tell her was that the children's charity was a PR exercise, set up to save face when the royal family had once again started losing traction with the citizens of Alouette. They'd set it up just after they'd introduced a raise in the tax rate, to increase the size of the grant that covered the monarchy's expenses.

'It's obvious to me that you love your siblings,' he said instead. 'What could have possibly happened for you to leave them behind?'

Gisele slipped her phone into the pocket of her dress

and turned her back on the view to face him. 'I would've thought that you'd know.'

He handed the drink to her. Red and orange liquids bled into each other, forming patterns around the crushed ice. The cold glass frosted with tiny water droplets and, when their fingers brushed, he was certain the spark from the touch would melt all the ice in the tall glass. 'It was easy to deduce that your parents would have treated you badly in some way or did something unforgivable.'

'I suppose they managed to quash any rumours about my departure.'

'Your parents rule the palace with fear. It would take a great deal to get anyone who works there to talk.' And yet Emilien had. He'd got information about his father's murder from a few members of the palace staff before smuggling them to another country, where they lived anonymously under his protection.

He watched Gisele play with the straw in her glass, hoping that she was trying to find the words to tell him exactly what had happened.

'Many things made me want to leave, Emilien,' she said, still not looking at him.

He'd allow her that. Whatever she was remembering was obviously difficult for her to talk about, but she was talking. She wasn't running, she wasn't pushing him away, so this was progress. It was a win.

'But there was a final straw.'

'Yes,' she breathed. 'Ten years ago my parents informed me that I was to marry King Héctor of Valonova. Claude was powerful, and would eventually take the throne so there was a great deal of focus on him. Me? I was less useful. The most useful thing I could do was to marry in order to secure power for our family.'

Emilien could feel a tremble start in his hands. A wick lit in his blood. He knew the king and queen were cruel, but how could they have treated their daughter like this?

'His children were just a little younger than me. We weren't friends, but I knew them. My parents wanted me to marry someone who was old enough to be my father. They had a plan to make my marriage to him more palatable for the masses. In their plan, I would marry when I was twenty-one, and then I would have his baby.'

That lit wick turned into a raging inferno. In that moment, Emilien wanted to take Gisele in his arms. He wanted to shield her with the violence of his anger. He wanted to tear the palace down more than ever, and he also wanted to tear down King Héctor for ever agreeing to this madness.

'A baby to solidify alliances,' he said. He could hear how his voice sounded; it was as if it had been scraped from the depths of hell.

'And so we'd have had a child with Bettencourt and Renaud blood, who would have power in Valonova.'

Emilien was burning alive. He could feel himself swaying and it had nothing to do with the movement of his docked yacht. Trying to cool his temper, he took a sip of his ice-cold drink, but it didn't work at all. 'So your parents wanted power in Valonova and you would be the one to secure it. Did they not consider that the reason Héctor wanted to marry you was for the very same reason?'

She leaned back against the metal rail and he could see the exhaustion in her shoulders. 'I don't think they expected him to be that audacious. They would have expected him to put the alliance first.'

'Yet *they* wouldn't have. What about Héctor's children? Would your parents have murdered them, like they did my father, for another throne?'

Gisele said nothing. All she did was raise her shoulders and let them drop. She clearly couldn't defend them.

Royals; they thought they were utterly untouchable. He would never trust one, not even this one. Which was why he had taken to calling her 'princess', even if her teeth ground every time he used it. The first time, it might have been used as a threat, but since their dinner it was a constant reminder to himself of exactly who she was, and why he could never soften towards her. It was a barrier he'd erected between them.

But he did want to protect her, and he did want to give her a chance for retribution. She was owed that much.

'This scheme, Emilien…' she said, finally looking at him. 'What if it doesn't work out between us? We barely know each other. I know it's supposed to be a year, but I don't want this marriage to become a prison.'

Emilien reached past her, placed his drink by the rail—a precarious spot, but he didn't care—and grasped her shoulders tenderly, hoping that she could see his sincerity even if she didn't quite trust him yet.

'If you wanted to leave, you would be free to. You'd always have a choice. Always.'

She nodded and took a step away, breaking the contact between them.

He didn't like that. He would have preferred it if she'd taken a step forward instead. How good would it feel to have her pressed against his chest? What would her hair smell like? How branding would that touch be compared to shaken hands and brushed fingers?

This wasn't the time to think about this maddening attraction. He needed to pay close attention to everything Gisele said and everything her body betrayed.

He watched her go back to the same spot she'd been

standing in before: by the railing, almost as if she'd decided that was the safest place for her to be. He couldn't deny that the space between them made it easier to think.

'I believe you,' she said finally, 'But I need to know why you believe there should be no love in this marriage.'

The naivety of the question startled him. 'Do you intend to fall in love with me, princess?' he asked, voice half-teasing, and was astonished to see her roll her eyes in the most un-princess-like manner.

Even more astonishingly, the sight made him smile. It felt as natural as taking a breath of air and yet completely alien at the same time. When had he last had anything to smile about?

The things they were discussing were entirely serious. He forced himself to focus on them. 'My parents loved each other fiercely and, when my father was killed, I saw how it broke my mother. She's never been whole since. I don't want that for myself, and I don't want to do that to anyone else. I learned a lesson from my father's death, Gisele, and that is that humans are terribly mortal. There's no escaping that fate. I *never* choose love.'

He watched Gisele move closer to him. It felt as if a force field had surrounded them and was only getting stronger. Then she lifted her hand and placed it on his cheek. He had no control at all when his body leaned into the touch.

'I'm so terribly sorry for everything my family has put you through. My heart breaks for you, Emilien.' She dropped her hand and shook her head, muttering to herself. 'I must be out of my mind.'

Emilien waited for the words that he wanted to hear. That he craved.

'I'll marry you.'

CHAPTER SIX

GISELE COULD BARELY believe the words had left her mouth, but she couldn't take them back now. She'd been so undecided when she'd climbed aboard this yacht and, right up until that second, still hadn't known what she would say. But hearing how much his parents had loved each other made her wonder how different his life could have been if her family hadn't destroyed it. She had to do something to make amends.

But, if she was being honest, that wasn't the only reason. That part of her which had always wanted to get back at her parents in some way wanted to agree to Emilien's plan. She had been treated so badly over those years she'd spent in the palace. Her self-esteem had been eroded daily by her mother's cutting remarks, the way that she'd never been quite enough in some ways and too much in others. She'd never been able to see any way she could exact any sort of vengeance on her own. With Emilien, however, possibilities existed.

And he was right. She might be able to speak to her siblings. If Emilien could hold her parents accountable for his father's death, if he could control them with the threat of making that information public—and a powerful man like Emilien who was this confident about his chances *must* have a way—then her alliance with him would allow her to make a few conditions of her own, such as having a relationship with Claude and Isabelle. What right did her parents have to keep her siblings away from her? Maybe then they could understand what it was to have no power. She wanted them to feel what she had for so many years.

So, while she wanted to help Emilien, she also recognised that she also had a very selfish reason for accepting his proposal.

Does this make me a bad person? Maybe she was. She'd always tried to do the right thing. The kind thing. But there was nothing kind in vengeance.

'I can see you over-thinking this decision, princess. Maybe we should go inside and talk about it.'

She looked at Emilien's outstretched hand. The afternoon sun smiled down on him like a spotlight, making him look divine. Dressed all in black. Was he a dark saviour or was he a demon disguised with a halo, one who would lead Gisele to her ruination?

Did it really matter? She was doing this for her freedom and her family.

She placed her hand in his and allowed him to lead her inside. 'Must you call me that?' she snapped, hating the word that reminded her of all her flaws. 'I'm not a princess any more. I was barely an adequate one. Princesses are perfect and I am *not*.'

They had entered a large, welcoming area that was obviously designed to entertain. There were large couches that looked so comfortable, they would undoubtedly be a trap where productivity died, because there was no way she could imagine getting off those cushions once she lay on them. A bar at the back end of the space with high, golden-legged stools tempted with strong drinks that were safely stored behind clear doors. A long dining table stretched along a large window that allowed a clear view of the blue waters. There were tables and chairs, and even a daybed, and the space was so light and bright, so completely at odds with Emilien's dark aura.

'Yes,' he replied, as he led her to a couch. 'Hiding or not, you still are one. And I wouldn't trust your family's judgment on adequacy. I'll be right back.'

She watched him disappear outside and return with their drinks, placing them on the table before taking his seat on the single chair set diagonally to her. He crossed his legs, ankle over knee. His arms poured over the cushioned arm rests. The black fabric of his formal shirt pulled taut across his torso, betraying the sculpture of the body beneath: the picture of elegance and power. Power he wore so casually, as if having so much influence over the world was his absolute right.

This show with his yacht, his money and his stories should have frightened her. Hell, the day before it would have, but not now. When she looked at him all she saw was a man who loved his parents deeply, and someone like that couldn't be all bad. Now when she looked at him all she felt was this powerful attraction that never went away. Now when she looked at him all she heard was a dark lullaby drawing her in.

Emilien sat there, running his finger along his bottom lip, hypnotising her, studying her. 'We need to discuss what comes next,' he finally said, breaking the spell he'd put her under.

'I'm listening.' She did her best to concentrate. If they were going to discuss terms of their marriage, she needed to pay close attention. She might admire Emilien, but she didn't trust him yet.

'The first thing is that we will be leaving for Alouette in two days.'

Gisele felt the blood drain from her face. Her heart rate increased. Her palms grew sweaty. Her mouth turned dry. She reached for her drink on the polished coffee table and took a long sip, but it did nothing to help. If anything, the cold of the ice felt shockingly violent against the heat that was suddenly pouring out of her entire body.

Then she felt Emilien beside her. He pulled the glass away from her, placed it elsewhere, grabbed her shoulders and turned her to face him.

'Look into my eyes,' he instructed. 'Breathe with me, princess. In through your nose, out through your mouth.'

She did as she was told, those remarkable hazel eyes grounding her to him. She kept her focus on his eyes, matching his breaths until the panic cleared from her mind and her heart rate started to slow.

'Good girl,' he praised. The words did something weird in her chest. 'You knew we would have to return,' he said.

'I know,' she replied shakily. 'But the thought of it…' She could picture her mother's face in her mind, her father's disinterested cruelty. 'I don't have to like it, okay?'

'Are you afraid?'

'Yes,' she admitted, looking away. Of course she was afraid. These people had had a man killed, they'd treated her badly and kept her siblings from her. Who knew what they would do to her when she went back?

Emilien grasped her, forcing her to look at him. 'I want you to listen to me very carefully. I promise to protect you and I never, *never* go back on my word.'

'I wish I could believe you, Emilien. I wish I could trust your word.'

'You'll learn to.'

He let go of her and she felt bereft of his touch. How easily he quietened the noise in her head. How quickly she craved more of this thing between them she'd never had before. But maybe space was a good idea. She stood and rounded the couch to stand at the window, gazing out at the water, at Saint-Lorin-de-la-Mer.

This place had been her sanctuary for ten years. Her shop was her pride and joy. Her flowers brought her happiness. The scent as she worked with them made her smile. Having people admire her creations made her proud. Every friendly word, waved greeting and little gift made her life here worth living. How could she know this existed and still manage to spend a year in Alouette? How would she do that when she had only bad memories of there?

She could feel Emilien watching silently. It was like a warmth cast on her back, but she refused to look at him, not when she was thinking about her shop. What would happen to Atelier Les Jardins while she was away? She'd built it from nothing. She was turning over handsome profits, but she still didn't employ anyone to take care of the management tasks for her because she loved doing that herself almost as much as she loved creating the arrangements. If she was gone, who would do all of that?

You have plenty of employees who can run the shop. You trained them yourself. That was true. Any one of her four employees could run the place. She trusted them immensely.

'It's natural to feel a bit of separation anxiety from your business,' Emilien said, making no move to come closer. 'But I have already promised to make it possible for you to manage things from Sineaux.'

'How do you do that?'

'Do what?'

'Anticipate everything I'm going to say or feel.'

'Maybe I just understand you, princess.'

She glanced at him. How she wished she could find someone who understood her. Emilien understood some things, but he'd never know what it felt like to crave affection, even if it was just from one person. He'd never understand what it felt like to have to consider moving away from the only people who had ever been good to her, even if it was temporary.

But it was just a year—twelve months. She could do that. And, afterwards, she would come back to Saint-Lorin-de-la-Mer and maybe this time, when her feet touched French soil, she would have Claude and Isabelle back in her life.

The thought gave her the strength to ask her next question. Turning to fully face Emilien, she clasped her hands in front of her and saw a shift on his face—almost as if he'd liked what he'd seen before but now she had displeased him in some way. A familiar crack formed in her chest. How was she failing this time? What had she done that was not good enough?

'What happens after we get to Sineaux?' she managed to ask, pushing through the pain.

'You will move in with me and then we start the arrangements for our wedding.'

The arrangement will be a mutually beneficial one. She would move in with him, live in his home. She wouldn't have to stay at the palace. Relief flooded her body, weakening her knees. But, knowing her parents the way she did, would they really allow that?

'What is it?'

'It's just that normally, before a royal wedding, the princess would be expected to live in the palace.'

Emilien stood and walked to her, each step sending a

shockwave through her belly, commanding her attention. He stopped so close to her that the front of his shirt almost touched the front of her dress. Large, warm hands gently cupped her face, tilting it up to his, and all she could see were those eyes. Eyes that had haunted her dreams since the first day she'd seen them.

'They can expect what they like, princess, but I will never let that happen. I promised to protect you; I'm not throwing you in the lion's den.'

Gisele had never felt so shielded as she as she did in that moment. It was as if nothing and no one could touch her. No one except the man who already did. He was doing nothing more than cradling her face, but the force of his touch spread out like a tingling web of sensation, catching on every surface of her body, turning her into an exposed wire, sparking and crackling. The feeling must have been contagious because it was reflected in his eyes too. They darkened and dipped down to her lips before snapping back to her eyes.

His lips pressed together, then his tongue darted out, licking the lower one, and Gisele could no longer breathe. She didn't *want* to, unless it was Emilien's breath she was breathing.

And maybe he anticipated what was going through her head again, because he leaned down towards her, a feat no one had ever managed before, because she was so tall. He stopped an inch from her lips. His breath whispered over her. Icy from the drink they'd shared. His scent: dark. Spicy, smoky and almost like leather, but there was a hint of something floral there too. Like a little secret she'd only just caught a whiff of.

Moments before all she'd known was that she needed to breathe his air; she'd had no idea that, when it happened, it would so totally consume her and kill every thought until there was just one: *Emilien.*

In her desperation to taste him, she uttered one breathy word. 'Please.'

And then his mouth was on hers. Crashing down and drowning her in a tsunami of unleashed passion. Cresting in the height of euphoria as his tongue touched hers and being sucked under in a sea of lust as his teeth scraped her lip.

That gentle caress on her face had changed. He had one hand with a firm grasp on the back of her neck, controlling this kiss, and the other moved to the small of her back, pressing her body against his. Her own hands fisted the front of his shirt in a desperate attempt to cling on for dear life as she absorbed wave after wave of pleasure so intense, it was unlike anything she had ever felt.

And then he tried pulling back just a little but she followed his lips with her own, and the sound torn free from his chest brought her to life in a way that was brand-new. It made her ravenous. Hungry for each one of his pleasure-filled tells. The window met her back as his body—so impossibly hard it told of the muscle beneath—pressed against hers. His tongue dancing with hers. He was just as lost as she was. His fingers were sinking into the soft flesh of her thighs, even though they were still over her clothes. His hands traced burning patterns as they moved all over her body. His muscles quivering from his restrained power.

This man was Hades and she wanted more. Her own hands found their way into his hair, grasping it in a tight hold that had him gasping out a raw, ragged, 'Fuck.'

He pulled away just slightly and she could scarcely believe what she had done. She hadn't meant to kiss this man but, from the moment she had seen him in his car outside her flower shop, she'd wondered what he would taste like.

Now she knew and nothing could have prepared her for this kind of passion, this kind of chemistry. It was primal.

And, when she looked at him and saw how hard he was breathing and how wide his pupils were, she knew he was feeling the very same thing.

CHAPTER SEVEN

Just as Emilien had planned, two days later they cruised to Alouette.

When they left the marina, Emilien insisted he accompany Gisele to her cabin himself. Why? He wasn't sure. All he knew was that he craved her presence. That kiss had messed with his mind. Even now he couldn't rid himself of the taste of her, the way she'd felt beneath him. The slope of her curves and softness of her skin, the fullness of her figure. With one kiss she had placed a spell on him, but it had been no ordinary kiss.

He never felt passion that explosive with anyone and he'd had plenty of experience in his thirty years. There was something about Gisele that was made for him, which was a particularly dangerous thought, since he didn't trust her and would never love her. Would never love anyone. Unfortunately, chemistry didn't require trust.

The only reason you don't trust her is because she's royalty.

And that was reason aplenty for him. She had affected him so powerfully from the very first moment he'd laid eyes on her that he had taken to calling her 'princess' as a constant reminder of who she was and what he had to do. That *she* wasn't important to him, revenge was.

He wasn't sure how efficiently that tactic was working now. Calling her princess brought a rush of heat through his body and a smile to his face. It was truly an irritation.

'After you,' he said, opening the door to a grand room situated close to his. Most of the space couldn't be seen from the door, because a floor-to-ceiling wall blocked the view, guaranteeing privacy. He ushered Gisele round the partition, noting the way her eyes widened as she took in the full effect of the cabin.

What appeared from the doorway to be a plain wall was in fact a huge black-and-ivory padded headboard against which there was a king-sized bed. And on either side of the bed stood a black nightstand. The whole cabin was decorated in greys, blacks, silver and ivory, with a thick grey carpet underfoot and a twinkling, modern chandelier hung from a glossy black panel above the bed. A modern *chaise* lay under the window that ran the length of the cabin's left side.

The bed itself faced glass doors which opened onto a private deck, from which Gisele would be able to see the aft of the yacht. Emilien could almost picture her standing out there, a soft, fluffy gown wrapped around her, a cup of coffee in her hands, a belt cinching in her waist, making those devastating curves all the more powerful.

He cleared his throat forcefully, easing the gruffness. '*En suite* is through those doors.'

'Thank you, Emilien.'

He nodded and left.

He'd given her the second-most luxurious room aboard the yacht. It was also the nearest to his, because he'd promised her protection, but now he seriously questioned the wisdom of placing her so close to him, because all he wanted to do was kiss her again, touch all the parts of her that were covered up by her clothes.

Maybe protection had been an excuse. Protection from whom? They would be virtually alone in the Mediterranean. He heaved a sigh to clear his head and went down to the lowest deck. Perhaps alone in the sun, with some work before him, he'd be able to shake Gisele from his thoughts.

It worked for a while. No matter what life threw at Emilien, he could always count on his job to distract him, drown out the noise. But when Gisele walked onto the deck, whatever focus he had found was lost. Shattered by her mere presence.

'Is there anything you need?' he asked, hoping she would take the hint and find somewhere else to be.

'No, I was just exploring.'

'If you require anything, feel free to ask the staff.'

'Thank you, I'll do that.'

He watched her walk further towards the back of the yacht, unable to tear his eyes away. She wore a dress today, a thin, flowy thing. Billowy on the arms and cinched in at her waist. The front was cut low with a string, the ends which hung down towards her full breasts, which were so temptingly emphasised by the style. The skirt caught around her legs, a fluttering flag in the wind. Her brown hair was swept to the side by the breeze, exposing her nape.

In that moment Emilien was sure he'd discovered astral projection because he was seated by his laptop, yet he could feel himself trailing his lips up her spine, over the back of her neck, inhaling her scent and placing open mouthed kisses…

'For heaven's sake!' he muttered under his breath. He needed to figure out what to do about this because being attracted to his wife was not an option.

She's not your wife yet.

A mere technicality.

'Emilien.'

He didn't have to shift his attention because he had already been so intently focused on her that, when she turned round, she immediately caught his gaze. He could see the moment that she fell into the same trap as he had, caught and held by their connection.

'Is there something I can help you with?' Determined to smother this attraction, he tried to shift focus onto whatever need Gisele might have.

She moved nervously, fingers fidgeting with the strings of her dress for a moment. Then she forced them to still, clasped them in front of her and pushed her shoulders back. He'd only known her a little while but, good Lord, he hated when she did that.

She'd done the very same thing two days ago when they'd been discussing the terms of their marriage. It was as if he was getting to see Gisele and understand her, and then in an instant she pulled the shutters down on the person she actually was and turned back into the princess. Into the royal. Reminding him so brutishly of who she was and the family she came from. He didn't like that it closed that window to her, keeping him out.

'I was just thinking…' she said. 'I know our marriage is just an agreement but maybe it wouldn't hurt to get to know each other just a little bit. I mean, we will be living together for a whole year. It would be nice to know who I'm living with.'

'So you want to get to know me.' He forced his lips to curve in a teasing smirk. The attraction was a frustrating distraction, but he would be lying if he said he didn't like teasing her just a little bit.

'Never mind. I shouldn't have said anything.' Gisele started to walk away, but Emilien closed his laptop and moved it to the side.

'Join me, princess.'

She stopped in her tracks, looking at him suspiciously for a moment, before she rolled her eyes and came to sit opposite him.

Emilien loved it when she did that. Maybe rolling her eyes was rude, but her exasperation was always amusing, and he couldn't imagine a princess of Alouette in that stuffy palace ever rolling her eyes at anyone. He wanted *that* Gisele to see the light of day. It was as though there were three different versions of her: the princess, the woman in hiding, living half a life, and the defiant woman she truly was.

'What would you like to know?' he asked indulgently.

She leaned forward, elbows on the table. 'Well, let's start with, are you from Sineaux?'

'Sinelaise through and through,' he answered.

'Even after...?' Gisele trailed off.

'After my father died?' He guessed her question.

Gisele nodded, eager for an answer.

'Yes. For a period my mother left town, but I remained in Sineaux and lived with my grandfather. At first she couldn't be near the society that seemed pleased my father was gone, but after about two years she returned. I had grown close to my grandfather who understood that, even though I was nobility, I wanted to have nothing to do with governing the country. So much so, that he left Talaria to me.'

'Talaria—the boats.' She propped her chin up on one hand, listening as if his life was the most fascinating thing she'd heard, and it made him want to do something he never did. It made him want to talk to her about his life, to confide in her.

He nodded.

'So this yacht was built by your company,' she said.

'Yes. Whenever I travel, as much as it is possible, I will use my yacht. When I drive, it's in my cars. When I buy or sell property, it's through my real estate company. When I need accommodation, it's in my hotels and resorts.'

'That would explain the car when you came to my shop.'

'The world knows I offer the best in luxury, so why wouldn't I want that for myself?'

Gisele laughed musically. Some people loved the sound of wind chimes, others the ocean or their favourite car— something that gave them goose bumps. Emilien had just found the sound that did that for him. He wanted to hear it again, record it and play it over and over.

'Have you always thought of yourself as the best?' Gisele asked.

'Wrong question. Have I always *known* that I am the best? And the answer is yes.'

She smiled, on the verge of laughing again. 'So conceited.'

'Conceited or do I just believe in myself?'

Just then his staff appeared and placed coffee, fruit and fresh croissants on the table between them. Due to how early he had wanted to depart, Emilien had instructed the staff to prepare a slightly later breakfast, thinking that Gisele would appreciate a meal once she'd had time to settle in her cabin. Clearly, she'd had different ideas.

He took a sip of his coffee, then plated some fruit for himself and her.

'So, now it's your turn,' he said. 'You've agreed to marry me so that you could see your siblings again. Is there no one else in Alouette that you would want to see or have back in your life?'

Gisele tried to hide the sadness in her eyes behind her coffee cup, and he let her, but clearly the answer was no.

'There was no one else,' she answered simply. 'I was never allowed to make friends of my own. I was forced to socialise with the children of nobles, who were cruel and cliquey. I didn't want to be around them when I lived in the palace; I certainly don't want to be around them now that I got out.'

'Fair enough.' A picture of Gisele as she had been in Alouette was starting to form in his mind. Ill-treated by her parents who owned her rather than loved her. Isolated. He was glad she'd found a way to escape. The alternative made fire course through his veins.

Gisele twirled the silver fork round in her hand before taking the tiniest of bites of her melon.

'If you don't like it,' Emilien said, 'I can instruct the chef to make you something else.'

'No! No, this is perfectly fine.'

But it clearly wasn't. He wouldn't say anything further on it, though. Gisele was an adult and capable of taking care of herself. If she said the food was fine, then the food was fine.

'We never discussed what being married would look like,' she said, still playing with her food. 'You're only marrying me for the seat in parliament. Does that mean you have other plans for companionship? Do you have a partner who's okay with this plan?'

'Princess, would you be okay with the person you are in a relationship with marrying someone else?'

'Of course not.'

'Then I think you have your answer.'

'So you're not in a relationship?'

'No, I am not.' He might be many things but a philanderer he was not. He'd grown up knowing what love and commitment looked like. At least he had, until he was thirteen. It bothered him that Gisele would question his integrity regardless of how innocently she did so.

'But why?'

'Should I be?'

'Isn't that what powerful men do? They live in the right places, they marry the right people, they have the correct number of children...'

'I don't do anything that is just expected of me without questioning it or it suiting me. I refuse to bow down to imaginary rules. The rules I set for myself are the only ones that matter.'

Gisele put her fork down, not that it had done much work. She had only taken a few nibbles of her melon. The rest of the plate remained untouched. 'Must be nice to have that kind of power.'

'Anyone can have that kind of power. Once the law is changed, you will have it too. If you wish to stay in Alouette, we can make that happen. Or, if you want to return to Saint-Lorin-de-la-Mer, I'll help you with that too.'

'Thank you, Emilien. I feel like I've said that a lot.'

'You don't need to. No one should have to live in a cage or live in fear.'

'No, no one should.'

Gisele drained her coffee cup and placed it politely back in the saucer. 'Thank you for breakfast. Please excuse me; I have some business to attend to.'

Gisele went up to her cabin. She spent the rest of the trip there, looking through the day's financials and making satin flowers to while away the hours. She had placed the assistant who had been with her longest in charge of managing Atelier Les Jardins. The arrangement would allow her to remain on top of things remotely while her assistant managed the operational aspects of the shop. She told herself this would be the reality anyway, if she one day decided to expand, and that helped her anxiety about leaving her store behind.

It was mid-afternoon when they arrived in Sineaux and docked at the harbour. A black Sylph car waited when they disembarked—a fancy sedan this time, rather than a sports car.

Emilien loaded their luggage into the boot before opening the door to the passenger side for her then, once she was in, closed it and rounded to the driver's side. Wordlessly, he drove them away from the water, but still along the coast, until they reached an area of the capital that was known for its huge mansions, high walls and fierce privacy. He pulled up to a gate, lowered the window with a single push of a button, then pressed his thumb to a reader. The solid gate swung open, allowing them to drive up a long driveway lined with tall trees that led to a stunning, entirely black villa made of glass and steel.

Most villas around the area invited the ocean in but not Emilien's. His home was like a jewel from the underworld placed in paradise. When he drove them into the underground parking garage, lined with rows of cars, the walls were black, the light warm. They walked inside his home, which was a beautiful artwork of swirling glass bannisters, with expertly lit paintworks in huge, gilded frames and sculptures, the place a canvas painted with the darkest colours Gisele had ever seen in a living space. It was all blacks, greys and charcoals with the odd pop of wood and tan leather. It was so masculine and modern, but so dark and broody.

Exactly like him: a man all in black in his black home. Unlike her home, which was filled with flowers at any given time. There were absolutely none here. Maybe she could bring in a few arrangements if she was to live here for the next year. It was only fair that she was at least a little comfortable, given that she wouldn't be here at all if it weren't for him.

She walked a little further into his home. She had to admit that the dark walls highlighted the splashes of colour from the artworks. Lifelike drawings of yachts and cars, and even a few of spectacular scenery, hung on the walls. They were different from the others. There was something emotional in the brush strokes.

'Who did these?' Whoever the artist was had incredible talent. They'd left their heart in these pictures.

'I did.'

Gisele's jaw dropped. 'These are incredible, Emilien! You're an artist?'

'No. I'm not.' There was an edge to his tone. 'I used to dabble a long time ago.'

'Wait, so you no longer draw?' That was a tragedy for him and the world.

'No.'

He picked up her suitcase and ascended the stairs, putting an end to the conversation. Why had he stopped? These were magnificent. A talent like this shouldn't go to waste. Gisele wanted to ask him more, but maybe that wasn't such a good idea when he clearly didn't want to talk about it.

Well, she had a year to convince him to draw again.

Having lost sight of him, she rushed up the stairs and

found him in a room that was just as monochromatic as the rest of the house, though still stunningly opulent.

'This will be your room for the year,' he said. 'You should get some rest. We'll be visiting my mother later.'

With that he turned round and closed the door, sealing her in this room with her thoughts running rampant, trying to figure out exactly who this man was under all his layers.

CHAPTER EIGHT

AN HOUR LATER they were on the road. Gisele, in the passenger seat, stole glances at Emilien, who kept his eyes firmly fixed ahead. Whatever ease they had found on the yacht had slipped away and now there was all this tension between them. Gisele wanted to know if she had done something wrong. Perhaps she had taken the questions about his art too far.

She hadn't missed this when she was in Saint-Lorin-de-la-Mer—this feeling of always wondering if she was doing the right thing. If she had done something wrong. If she was enough. If she looked just right. When she was in her own home, none of that mattered.

'When we get there, you are not to reveal why we're getting married.'

'You want me to lie to your mother?' she asked, surprised that Emilien would want to do such a thing when he clearly cared for her.

'I expect you to act as my fiancée.'

'Why don't you want her to know?'

'I would never deprive my mother of the joy it would bring her to see me wed. I know it's something she's wanted for me, and worry in any form isn't good for her health, so we will keep the truth from her.'

'Why isn't it good for her health?'

Emilien squeezed the steering wheel, his nostrils flaring. Were her questions really that frustrating?

'She has cardiovascular disease, so I try to keep her life as calm as possible and...'

'And?' Gisele urged.

'She's battled depression for a long time. The last thing I want to do is cause her any more strife or give her a reason to spiral.'

'Okay,' Gisele agreed. Emilien didn't have to say when the depression had started. She could guess.

They arrived at yet another villa, but this one was the polar opposite of Emilien's. This one was light and bright, the kind of place she expected to see along the cliffs off Sineaux. Once they parked and walked up a stone path, he let them into the quiet house.

'Does she live here alone?' Gisele asked.

'No,' he replied. 'It would be far too dangerous for that. I have medical staff on hand twenty-four-seven.'

It was quite the commitment to provide that kind of round-the-clock care. Something she would have expected at a private clinic that was so popular amongst the rich.

'Come on.' Emilien took her hand in his and she watched his jaw work as that spark between them flared to life. He hadn't touched her since their kiss and now, with his hand in hers, the feeling of that kiss was brought back in bright Technicolor.

'She'll be outside,' Emilien said, his voice lower than before.

'You say that like she shouldn't be.' Gisele almost laughed at the nearly parental tone he'd used.

'That's because she shouldn't.'

Gisele simply shook her head and allowed him to lead

her wherever they were going. It turned out they were heading out onto a terrace. Out by the pool on a lounger under a wide patio umbrella lay a beautiful woman with bright blonde hair in a colourful kaftan.

'Mama, should you really be lying in the sun?'

'Emilien, I have so few pleasures left in life, would you really take this from me?'

Emilien sighed. 'You're being dramatic. I'm concerned about your health. If I'd known you'd be so stubborn I'd have got you an apartment.'

'You wouldn't dare, *mon fils*.'

'Wouldn't I?'

'No, you wouldn't,' his mother insisted. She got off the lounger and Gisele saw that she shared the same remarkable hazel eyes as Emilien's. Her face, though, was decorated with the creases of her years. It didn't detract from her beauty. It emphasised the beauty of ageing gracefully.

'Mama, I'd like you to meet my fiancée.'

The shock on Camille's face as she looked between Emilien and her almost made Gisele laugh. Clearly, she had no idea that Emilien was seeing anyone, and why would she? He had told Gisele he hadn't been in a relationship.

'What did you do, *mon cœur*?'

'Asked her to marry me, obviously.'

She tried so hard but Gisele couldn't stop the giggle that erupted from her lips then, and instantly she had two burning Montagne gazes snapping in her direction.

'Seeing as how my fiancé is being so rude,' she said, smiling, 'Let me introduce myself. I'm Gisele Bettencourt.'

'Bettencourt?' his mother said accusingly at her son. All amusement and humour went from her face, replaced by something angry.

'She's not like them, Mama,' Emilien said, defensively. '*Mon amour*, this is my mother, Camille Montagne.'

'It's very good to meet you.' Gisele extended her hand, but Camille just looked at it with disgust.

'Mama,' Emilien warned.

'It's okay, *mon loup*.' Gisele looked up at him, hoping she was doing a good job convincing everyone of her role as the loving fiancée. The nickname came naturally. It was entirely fitting for who he was. A wolf. She wasn't sure if he would approve of her calling him that but, considering he persisted in calling her princess even though she made no effort at hiding how much she hated it, she couldn't bring herself to care.

'I understand your reservations, Camille, but with time you'll see that Emilien and I really do care for each other.'

There was no lie there. She did care about him. She cared enough to agree to his plan so that he could have his revenge—even though he still hadn't been open about his schemes—but also so that she could have her siblings back in her life. It was a mutually beneficial agreement; that didn't mean that there wasn't something else here. Even on the yacht he'd promised to help her settle into whatever life she chose for herself. He didn't have to do that, not unless he cared.

'You care about my son?' Camille said, her eyes narrowed.

'Of course I do.'

'We'll see about that.'

'Mama, behave.' Emilien's hand left Gisele's and instead his arm wrapped around her waist, pulling her closer to his side. There was so much more of their bodies in contact now. She looked up at him just as he looked down at her, their gazes colliding with the power to erase everything around them. The stunning view. The magnificent villa. Even Camille. All gone in an instant.

'This is all very quick, Emilien. I saw you two weeks ago and now you're engaged.' When Gisele forced herself to look back towards the older woman, she found Camille's attention had turned to her hand. 'Where is the ring?'

'Oh…um…' Gisele didn't have an answer. Emilien hadn't told her what to say if it came up and, honestly, she should have thought of it herself.

'I am taking her to the jeweller so that she can pick one out for herself.'

'That seems very convenient, *mon fils*.'

'Or I know my fiancée and I'd like to give her a choice when she's had very few in her life.'

Gisele knew Emilien was playing a part. She knew that there wasn't anything real between them, but those words wormed their way into her heart, and she so badly wished they were true, because they were perfect.

She cleared her throat, hoping her voice didn't sound as emotional as she felt. 'Perhaps I should get us some drinks.'

'That sounds like a good idea, *mon amour*.' Emilien kissed the top of her head which made everything in her body tense and melt at the same time. She walked away, trailing her hand over his back, and felt his muscles stiffen. The fact that he couldn't hide that her touch affected him made Gisele feel powerful.

She went inside and found the kitchen, where a cook stood at the stove, preparing a meal.

'Can I help you, *mademoiselle*?' the man asked.

'I just need to get some drinks.'

'Of course. Let me get that for you.'

'Thank you.' She went to the window, where she realised she could see out to the pool area, and watched Emilien silently. She understood his mother's apprehension. After all her family had done to the Montagnes, it was probably a win that Camille hadn't thrown her out altogether. But that part of her that had been so worn down by her own parents was breaking apart, because yet again someone had found her lacking. She would never be enough, not for anyone. That seemed to be the lesson life kept teaching her.

There was something inherently wrong in her make-up, and she wondered why the universe would concentrate all of that into one person. What had she done in a past life that was so awful that she had to live this one? She silently stood by the window, watching him hug his mother, saying words she couldn't hear. She watched him ease Camille back down onto the lounger and sit on the side of the one next to it. His elbows rested on his knees, hands clasped together, leaning towards Camille and nodding as she spoke.

And then she saw him smile. Gisele tried to get even closer to the window, pressing her hands on the sill. The smile was so unlike any of the ones he'd given her, the teasing smirks. This was pure and unguarded and, if she'd thought he was breathtaking before, she wasn't prepared for what he looked like now.

'He loves his mama,' the cook said, startling her. Gisele glanced at the man briefly, before looking back at Emilien. She couldn't resist another sight of that look on his face.

'He bought this place for her,' the cook went on, 'And had it completely redone, then he hired all of us, because he didn't want her to be in some facility, no matter how luxurious. He knew she'd be happier here. She loves the water, you see, so he found her somewhere private she could enjoy it all by herself. He's a good son.'

Gisele hoarded away every scrap of the information the talkative employee let fall, hungry for anything that helped her understand the man outside better. 'Yes, he is,' she agreed.

Forcing herself to turn around, she found that the cook had prepared a tray of drinks.

'You can go outside,' he said. 'I'll have someone bring this out to you.'

'Don't be silly, I'm here now.' Gisele picked up the tray and went back to the pool terrace, steeling herself for whatever Camille might say next. She placed the tray on the stone table shaped like an hourglass that stood between the lounges, handed a glass to Camille, then one to Emilien. Then she took her own and sat beside him, linking her arm in his and resting her head on his shoulder.

Yes, they were playing a role, but this felt so easy. So right. When he leaned his head on hers, she felt complete. This was what she had wanted when she'd run away from Alouette. How strange she should find it with the person she shouldn't want.

'Are you okay?'

She thought Emilien was asking his mother at first but, when she felt his head leave hers, she glanced up to find him looking at her.

'Oh, yes. I'm fine. Are you?'

'I'm always fine when you're around, *mon amour.*'

She caught Camille studying the two of them.

'It's beautiful here,' Gisele offered, hoping to have some pleasant conversation.

'Yes, it is. So you're the lost princess.' Camille would not be distracted. She was almost as single-minded as her son. 'Where have you been all this time?'

'In France,' Gisele answered. 'I'm a florist in Saint-Lorin-de-la-Mer.'

'A florist, you say.'

'She's being humble. She's the best florist in the south of France.'

'I have a good team,' Gisele said, looking up at Emilien. She would never have been as successful, or able to focus on the creative side of the business, if she hadn't had the employees she did. They made Atelier Les Jardins work.

Emilien grasped her chin in that way he did when he wanted her to accept something he said as an undeniable truth. The touch took her breath away just as it always did. 'A team is only as good as the one leading it.'

Gisele could think of nothing to say to that.

'Why a florist?' Camille had a small smile on her face as she asked the question.

'Because flowers are honest and beautiful and all they have to do is exist to make the world better.'

'Which is very unlike palace life,' Camille added.

'Precisely.'

'I understand,' Camille said. 'I too left society life and its Machiavellian tendencies.'

'It's exhausting and cruel.' Gisele felt a lump form in her throat. No one in her life had understood how she felt and now, having found someone who shared her feelings, she felt a sense of peace overcome her. The tension she usually held in her body when she spoke to people ebbed away.

'Very much so. I'm glad you got out, Gisele.'

'Me too, Camille.' Gisele offered the older woman a smile and, when it was returned, she knew that the tide of Camille's dislike was turning.

'We came here because we have something to tell you,' Emilien informed her. There was a softness in his eyes that she mourned the loss of when he turned towards his mother. 'We will be holding our wedding soon, and you will be a witness.'

'You know, *mon fils*, ordinarily a person would ask.'

Gisele couldn't help grinning. 'But he's no ordinary person.'

'No, he's not,' Camille replied. 'I would be happy to.'

'Good,' Emilien said.

'Won't you both stay for dinner?' Camille asked hopefully, proof that Gisele had won over Emilien's mother.

'Oh no, we couldn't impose.' Gisele had no idea what the chef had prepared. Would it even be something she should be eating?

'It's no imposition.'

'Really, we couldn't, and truth be told I'm not very hungry,' Gisele lied.

'You haven't eaten today, *mon amour*,' Emilien said, betraying her. She wanted to elbow him in the ribs but that wouldn't escape Camille's notice.

'We should be leaving, *mon loup*,' she said instead.

'I suppose you're right. We have a lot to do.' He held out his hand towards her as he stood and she took it, offering him a beaming smile in gratitude. With her other, she grasped Camille's in farewell.

'It was lovely meeting you, Camille.'

'And you, Gisele. Welcome to our family.'

'Thank you,' she said through a lump in her throat.

Emilien led her back to the car in silence. Only once they'd got into it did he speak. 'You did well today.'

Unsure how to process the praise, Gisele didn't respond, but she couldn't help staring at Emilien, putting together the pieces she'd collected. A dedicated son. A genius at business. A talented artist. Those were all the things in the light. But there were other parts of him that were cast in absolute darkness. This need for revenge. His determination. His intensity. The former were obviously born of the love in his family, but the latter? Those came from the death of his father.

And yet the dark parts of him didn't make him less. They just made him the person he was. It made the good in him shine brighter, and there was so much good. How would Gisele spend a whole year with him, knowing all this, and not let him into her heart?

Perhaps the fact that she couldn't trust him would keep her safe. After all, all his moves were made on a chessboard that no one else had a complete view of. Even today, he hadn't been honest with his mother, though he loved her so completely.

Gisele could never expect honesty towards her either. And she would just have to remember that.

CHAPTER NINE

GISELE FIXED A tennis bracelet around her wrist, the stones as blue as the water surrounding the private island they were on. Camille had lent it to her. This one piece of jewellery was her something old, borrowed and blue.

It was her wedding day. A wedding that she was still conflicted about. It wasn't the fairy tale she had hoped to have when she'd been younger, but that morning ten years ago when her parents had tried to bind her to King Héctor was the day that fairy tales had died.

This wedding was a step in getting Claude and Isabelle back and hopefully making her parents pay for hurting so many people.

She looked around the suite she was in. It was bright and gauzy, beautiful beyond imagination. Every piece of furniture was so perfectly considered to complement all the nature around them and the sea beyond. The wood reminded her of sea-bleached driftwood. The canopy and sheer curtains making it romantic.

Even though she was surrounded by so much beauty all she could think was that she was so completely alone on her wedding day. Emilien had had a make-up artist and a stylist come in to pamper her in the lead-up to walking down the aisle, but even they had now left. It was a stark reminder of what she had in her life and that was her shop. Now that it had been temporarily taken away, she had nothing.

Gisele walked to the full-length mirror in the corner of the room, taking in her appearance as a bride. This dress was magnificent. She wasn't entirely sure how Emilien had managed it, but within days she'd had a designer dress perfectly fitted to her full figure—an off-white diaphanous creation making her look more an ethereal being than human bride.

Caught in the light, she could catch only the barest glimpse of the shape of her body beneath all the fabric, fabric that fell like a flowing waterfall. A single sheer layer covered her arms, went over her shoulders and joined the cape at her back which eliminated the need for a train or veil. And from her neck down to her thighs was a work of the most spectacular embroidery of blush-pink flowers and silver-green leaves with the tiniest crystals sewn into the eye of each flower and the vein of each leaf. The floral pattern repeated along the bottom edge of her dress upwards in an artistic gradient. A thin ribbon encircled her waist, and for the very first time in her life Gisele could appreciate her body and its hourglass shape.

This dress was an ode to who she was now. To her shop and her love of flowers. There wasn't a single royal colour in sight, and she was very grateful to Emilien for making this happen.

Then she looked at the ring on her finger. After they had left Camille's home, he had taken her to a jeweller who had opened up shop after hours just for Emilien. He had taken them to a secondary room with jewellery far more exquisite and a lot more pricey than anything out front. It was there that she had found this ring. The arms of the band stretched in a vine pattern. The tiny flowers between the gold leaves had a small emerald in the centre of each one, and the vines wrapped over the top and bottom edge of a brilliantly cut oval diamond.

Gisele didn't know what life would hold after this year, but something told her this was likely to be the only engagement ring she'd ever receive, so at least it was perfect.

She went to the bed and picked up her bouquet: a mix of black-star lilies, black roses and black dahlias. A positively gothic choice with which to walk down the aisle, but they so perfectly suited Emilien, and she could see no better way to show him that she was committed to their plan than to carry a bit of him with her.

They were on one of his private island resorts, a highly intimate venue with only five villas. Trees and vegetation worked around all the buildings, pools and courts. Emilien had told her to choose whatever flowers she wanted. It didn't matter what they were, he'd source them. He was always so sure of himself that part of her had wanted to test him a little.

She ran her finger along the edge of one of the black-star lilies. She'd placed this very flower on her list partly because it would have to be flown in from South Africa, and Emilien had succeeded in her impossible task. It had been a test to see if he could deliver on all the promises he kept making. The promise that he'd be able to protect her from anything. That he had the power to do whatever he wanted. Well, she had the proof in her hand.

'Come on, Gisele, time to get married,' she told herself. 'There's no turning back now.'

She pictured Emilien, what he would look like waiting for her at the altar, and she really didn't want to turn back.

She took one last look at the room behind her before

she stepped out of the door and made her way to the private beach.

The biggest runner she had ever seen ran on the ground from the edge of the pool deck, down onto the sand and all the way to Emilien. He stood by an arch draped with flowers and flowy white fabric. She couldn't quite make out his face from this distance but still her heart fluttered.

There was no music to walk down the aisle to. They didn't need any. The only people in attendance were the celebrant, his mother, his PA and a photographer, who hovered around. Gisele had no one to give her away. She wondered whether, if Claude had still been in her life, he would have wanted to take on that role. Because she certainly didn't want her father. In her dreams, Isabelle would have been by her side as her maid of honour.

The thought of her brother and sister settled any remaining nerves. She straightened her shoulders and took a step off the deck towards Emilien. In a few minutes he would be her husband and she could not have chosen a more beautiful man. He stood there in a burgundy suit, the lapels black. A matching waistcoat beneath and, under that, a crisp white shirt and an ebony tie. He'd never looked more dark and enticing and utterly breathtaking than in that moment. She didn't have to force herself to take the next steps. His presence drew her forward, her feet barely touching the ground as she glided towards him.

And then she saw, in his lapel, a blush-pink rose.

He hadn't wanted her to choose his *boutonnière*. He'd wanted to do it himself. Now she knew why. She was taken back to their first meeting when she'd held a rose so tightly in her hand that it had drawn blood. A pink rose.

And wasn't it amazing that Emilien had chosen to show

her that they were a team in the exact same way she had done, with flowers? Maybe this year wouldn't be so bad.

Emilien stood at the altar waiting for Gisele. His mother and his PA sat on either side of the aisle, the only two guests at his wedding, but he didn't really look at them. He kept his gaze firmly focused on where his bride would appear and walk to him, down an aisle lined with bright, beautiful flowers just like the kind he had seen at her shop. Each arrangement was dotted with blooms that ranged from the deepest maroon to the darkest of black, ones that he wouldn't have known the names of had it not been for Gisele's list.

When the minute hand reached exactly twelve, she appeared.

The morning sun forced its way through the trees, casting its golden light over her. With her chestnut hair tied up and a ribbon placed over the top like a headband, she looked like a Greek goddess. Then she started walking towards him and his lungs ceased working. With each step she took, he wanted to run towards her. Pick her up. Hold her against his body. He wanted to tell everyone to leave and never come back. He wanted to crush his lips to hers and worship at her feet.

But that was not what this marriage would be. This marriage was a means to an end, and he would *not* grow attached to his wife. But he couldn't deny the violence of his attraction towards her when she silenced the ocean, for heaven's sake! Would he have to fight this for the whole year? Could he grow some sort of immunity to it?

And then she was right in front of him, holding her dark bouquet. As dark as his suit. As dark as his home.

'Beautiful.' His voice was scraped raw. Damn this woman!

She offered him a smile in return and his mother stepped up to take the bouquet from her, allowing Gisele to place her hand in his. It took all his willpower not to grasp it tightly, pull her into him and kiss her, ravishing her lips in front of all these people. Her warm brown eyes held a heat too, as if she read his mind.

Man, were they in trouble!

The celebrant began speaking. Emilien knew the course the ceremony would take. First, the man would welcome all two of their guests, then he would say what marriage should be and then he would talk about the importance of their vows. But Emilien couldn't pay any attention to the actual words. Not when Gisele was looking directly into his eyes.

She made the world disappear when they touched. He thought of nothing else. His mind was quiet for once. Nothing else existed.

'Pay attention,' she mouthed, clearly fighting back a smile, and he wished she would just let it fly. She had good reason for saying that, though, because everyone was waiting for him.

'Repeat after me,' the celebrant said, and so Emilien did. He slipped the rose-gold wedding band in the shape of a vine onto Gisele's finger, saying those traditional vows and knowing they were just words. They meant nothing without actions. Actions that he would not be taking, because he only needed to get married for that parliamentary seat. The only vows that were important to him were the ones he'd already made to Gisele to protect her and help her get her siblings back.

He let go of her hand and then she was saying the same

vows to him as she pushed a plain platinum band over the knuckle of his finger.

'By the power vested in me by the Kingdom of Alouette, I now pronounce you husband and wife. You may now kiss the bride.'

Emilien had planned to place a chaste kiss on her lips but he should have known better, because there was no controlling this passion between them when it had somewhere to go. The moment his lips touched hers, he was lost. Lost to the desperation and chemistry, to the storm of lust she ignited within him. She kissed with a hunger that told a story of someone who had tasted passion and craved more. Someone who was teased with a hint of something that tasted like ambrosia and, now that they'd had a taste, they wanted it all. And Emilien wanted to give it to her, but not here. Not in front of his mother, his PA and the celebrant.

Husband and convenient wife, a voice at the back of his mind said. A voice that allowed him to pull away and witness the shock on Gisele's face.

Her chest rose and fell. It was like that moment on the yacht all over again. Emilien knew now more than ever that he was going to have to find a way to keep his distance from his very beautiful wife because she had the power to distract him from everything.

CHAPTER TEN

KEEP HIS DISTANCE? An impossible task when they were on their way to their honeymoon.

'I thought we were honeymooning where we married,' Gisele said, as the polished wooden speedboat they'd boarded immediately after the ceremony planed through the calm ocean waters.

Emilien had strapped his new wife into the seat closest to him and could still feel her body under his hands. 'No, we're going somewhere even more exclusive.'

'Another resort owned by Montagne Holdings, I'm assuming.' A few tendrils of hair had blown free from Gisele's hair style. How could one person be so strikingly beautiful?

Emilien forced himself to focus on steering the boat. Once they arrived, he could have a little bit of separation from her. 'You would assume correctly.'

'What was wrong with the place we were just at?' she asked.

'Well, considering you have been away for ten years, have not yet been to the palace and we just had a photographer taking pictures of our wedding that'll soon be all over the Internet, I'm assuming that the palace would send someone there shortly. Now, we could go where I've planned, have a few quiet days and let them stew, or I can turn the boat around and you can meet your family sooner.'

He didn't like the idea of her being anywhere near the royals. As much as she wanted to see her siblings, they hadn't made any attempt to contact her and her parents were vile. But, if she chose the latter, he would take her back and he would stay with her, even if proximity to her made his life difficult.

'I'm happy to see what you've planned,' Gisele said, looking slightly pale.

'That's what I thought.'

'So how much more exclusive could this place be?' She was being a lot more talkative than usual, but Emilien was enjoying it, just as he'd enjoyed seeing her interact with his mother. The patience and understanding with which Gisele had handled Camille, and the acceptance his mother had shown, had all created a want in him to have his new bride with him at every visit. And, when she had called him her 'wolf', he'd wanted to hear it again. But how could he want something like that with someone he could never fully trust?

These new needs were intolerable. He wouldn't allow Gisele to soften his defences. He would not love her or make himself vulnerable to her.

'You really don't like surprises, do you?' Emilien was constantly learning things about Gisele, things that his fact file couldn't cover, and he liked it, which further highlighted how problematic her presence was.

'In my experience, surprises are usually a bad thing.'

'Like the surprise you'd have to marry a king.' He could only imagine what else she'd had to deal with in her previous life.

'Precisely. I'd much rather be told everything up front. That way, I can prepare myself.'

'Or prepare to flee.' He glanced back to see her nod. 'Well, princess, can you offer me this little bit of trust? I think you'll like the surprise. There are no forced weddings at the end of it.'

'No, that happened an hour ago.'

The barb struck. Had he really forced her to marry him? As far as he was concerned, he had given her a choice and she had chosen to become his wife. She had her own reasons for doing so. He was nothing like her parents, who would have forced her to marry someone so much older and consigned her to a life of being nothing more than a fancy hostage.

'And, yes, I can offer you that much trust,' Gisele went on.

The words brought him a small amount of relief, but he didn't respond.

A group of islands appeared on the horizon. Emilien owned several in the archipelago off the coast of Sineaux, one of which he'd used for their wedding. Most of the others offered luxury retreats for the rich and famous but those weren't the ones he'd take her to.

'To answer your question from earlier, it can get a lot more exclusive. The island we're going to has only one villa on it.'

'I can imagine what that would cost.'

'People are always looking for privacy and they pay a premium to have it. I know how to make that premium worth it.'

'I know. I looked you up.'

'Did you find anything interesting?' He glanced back at her.

'Plenty. But getting to know you like this is far more interesting, *mon loup*.'

There was that nickname again. He gripped the wheel even tighter then and slowed the boat down as they approached the island and docked the light vessel in the boat house. Once it was securely tethered, he stepped out and took Gisele's hand, helping her disembark and leading her up the staircase onto a path that took them towards the villa. There were plants everywhere. Rock gardens, streams and paved walkways. The entire place was landscaped to look like a wild, forgotten hideaway but every detail was deliberate.

'What's that building over there?' Gisele pointed out a building similar in design to the villa but plainer and more restrained.

'Staff quarters,' he answered. 'Visitors have the options of having the villa fully serviced, a private butler or renting it without any staff, in which case one would be completely alone on the island.'

'Are we alone?'

'Of course. But there is a spa and sauna here. If you wish to use any of the facilities, let me know and I'll have staff arrive to tend to you.'

'And then they would leave?'

'Yes.' Emilien didn't often stay at this resort but it was his favourite. The villa itself was built on the water where it was deepest and a wooden walkway connected it to the island.

'You can have a look around in a moment,' he said when he let them inside. 'There are few things to take care of first.'

'Like what?'

'Like this.' He made sure she was following him as he

went down a set of spiral stairs. The wooden platform and twinkling waters outside disappeared as they descended further. A glass wall beside them turned everything blue as they ventured beneath the water's surface, allowing them to peer into another world.

'This is amazing,' Gisele breathed.

'It gets better.' They stepped off the stairs and passed through an archway into an enormous tubular bedroom. The domed ceiling that also acted as the walls was entirely clear.

Emilien didn't look at his surroundings. He was fascinated by the wonder on Gisele's face as she looked up and a school of fish passed overhead. She went to the panel at the foot of the bed, putting fingers to the acrylic, almost as if she wanted to touch the coral that spread out beyond it in myriad colours.

'It's impressive,' Emilien said smugly. He was being honest. He himself was impressed by it every time he came here.

'I want to call you out for being conceited, but honestly, you're right. I've never seen anything like this.'

'You can admire it all you want. This will be your bedroom, and there's a sitting area just through there,' he said, pointing at another archway. 'First I need you to come with me.'

She stood at the wall just a moment longer before reluctantly following him into a walk-in wardrobe without that spectacular view. It made up for that lack by being larger than most bedrooms and the fittings made it look like a high-end store. It was filled with clothes.

'These are for you,' he said, standing beside racks off dresses, coats, skirts and trousers.

'Emilien, what is all this?'

He watched her walk towards the garments slowly, as if her feet were treading through treacle. She touched the sleeve of something that was silver and embellished.

'Now that you're back in Alouette, you're going to need a wardrobe befitting a princess. There's nothing wrong with the clothes you own…' Heaven knew, they drove him wild. 'But they're not the outfits of a royal. We are both high profile individuals and now we have to be prepared for the scrutiny that comes with it.'

'I didn't miss that.' There was a catch in her throat that made his heart break for her, but this was all part of the plan, and there would be no deviating from that plan, ever. Still, he could offer her comfort.

And yet, as soon as the thought had formed, he stopped himself from following through on it, because they were entirely alone here. And, if he offered her comfort, what would come next?

Thankfully his phone vibrating saved him from having to say or do anything.

'I have to take this.'

'I understand. Thank you for this. It's very considerate.'

He walked out of the room but rejected the call. He knew exactly who it was, and he wanted to make the royals sweat. While they were on the boat a message had come through informing him that the pictures of the wedding had gone live, which meant it would be only a matter of time before someone from the palace would see them. They likely already knew Gisele was in the kingdom. By the time he went upstairs to the guest room where he would be sleeping—a room with the second-best view—there was an email waiting in his inbox. He opened it and saw that it was a summons to the palace, exactly as he'd anticipated.

He quickly typed out a response:

I am honoured by your invitation and will consider accepting upon my return from my honeymoon.

He sent the reply, knowing no one turned the king and queen down. It was a blatant power play on his end to say that he would only consider it, but he wouldn't scrape and bow to murderers.

Emilien sent instructions to his PA to ensure no one from the palace was pencilled into his diary and that none of them were to be in contact with his mother either. Once he was certain that they would all be fully barred from any property he owned, he went in search of his new wife.

He was pleased to find her on the island, sitting by the poolside. But, when he got closer, he noticed that despite the heat, and even though her feet were dangling in the water, she had a sarong firmly tied around herself. Not just around her waist, but around her body, tied at the back of her neck like a dress. It was odd but he let her be. After all, she was only just married to him and maybe she wasn't comfortable with him yet.

The thought didn't sit right with him, but he opted to give her space. After all, hadn't he already made up his mind to keep his distance? Perhaps her covering up was in their best interests—for Gisele's comfort and for his willpower to stay away and ignore this potent want.

Over the next few days, a routine emerged. Gisele, like him, awoke early. They shared breakfast and, while Emilien worked, she found some way to entertain herself. But every day she covered herself with large sarongs, kaftans or kimonos. Good Lord, he wanted to take them off her! She was so beautiful, it was driving him insane. And, with the kiss they'd shared on the yacht and the one at the altar constantly on his mind, his body craved to take her. He wanted it so badly, it was a need that was nearly painful. It consumed him every single day.

But after five days of the same routine, the same outfits, it wasn't only his need that weighed on his mind. He pushed away from the desk in the small office space and went to the window from which he could see Gisele at the pool once again. He pulled the glasses that he only used while working on his computer from his face and let them dangle in his fingers.

The thought about Gisele's discomfort around him had occurred several times over the time they'd spent there. Each time, he liked it less and less. He wanted to ask about it. Wanted her to talk to him and be open with him, even though he knew he would never do the same, because he couldn't give her his trust, and asking questions like that would be to demand hers.

Of course, that was hypocritical of him, but she was a royal and he couldn't trust a royal. It was something he would never get past. He, on the other hand, had offered her freedom. If there was anyone more trustworthy in this partnership, it was him.

If that were true, wouldn't she have confided in you already?

Not necessarily. At one point in her life, Gisele had wanted a marriage with love, but she was no longer that hopeful romantic. Instead, she'd become pragmatic and maybe she saw no reason to confide in a man who was only temporarily in her life.

Crack!

He looked down to find his glasses crushed in his grip.

'Damn it!' He went back to the glass-and-steel desk, disposing of the bent metal and broken lenses. Why had he had such a strong reaction to the thought of her leaving?

That was meant to be the plan—that this marriage was a convenient arrangement that would one day end. Without love, what else could it be? And he certainly wasn't going to fall in love with her. There was zero danger of that happening. Princess or not. He wouldn't allow himself to turn into someone like his mother, someone who would deliberately put themselves in a vulnerable position, which was exactly what loving someone did. Making that choice would be insanity.

However, that didn't mean he couldn't offer her kindness.

He went to his room and changed out of his suit into swim shorts, then went to the pool deck, where Gisele lay on a lounger. It had become her favourite spot apart from the sitting area in the underwater room. The evening sun cast brilliant shadows around her, rays catching her brown eyes, bringing a new life to them. Cognac and glass and fire and sunsets all flashed in his mind. Gisele's eyes, lit by the sun, were a colour he felt in his heart.

'Would you like to join me for a swim, princess?'

'A swim?'

'Come now, don't look so surprised. We're surrounded by water,' he said, coming to stand at the foot of her lounger.

'I'm astounded you're not working,' she replied.

But that was not the only thing that had her surprise. He could tell she kept forcing herself to look into his eyes when hers kept trailing over his body.

'See something you like?' he teased.

'Shut up, Emilien,' she mumbled grouchily, turning red, and he barked out laughter. Once he'd started, he found he couldn't stop, his shoulders shaking and his stomach hurting at her look of good-natured outrage. He hadn't laughed like it in years, but the sight of an embarrassed Gisele was extraordinarily endearing.

'Come on,' he urged. 'It's just a pool. The water will be lovely.'

'No, it's quite alright. You go right ahead; this book is very absorbing.'

'You had the same amount read this morning as you do now. It can't be that interesting.'

'How did you know that?'

'Do you think that I haven't been paying attention?' It seemed ridiculous, when he'd been paying attention to every little thing she did, every minute movement she made. He sat on the lounger beside her. 'I see the way you look at the water and yet you've made no attempt to go in. You cover up in these every day,' he said, touching the silky fabric of the kimono she wore today. 'Talk to me. Tell me what's going on.'

She closed her book and placed it on her lap, looking away. Her lips curved at the corners and she swallowed thickly. Emilien tried to look at her face, but she wouldn't allow him to, and he was almost certain if she did he would find the sheen of tears in her eyes.

'Look at me, Emilien.'

He had been looking. He'd been looking since he'd first seen her. He couldn't stop looking.

'Princess, you're beautiful.'

But she shook her head.

'This is because of something your parents said to you, isn't it?'

'Growing up, they were very critical of me. They wanted me to behave a certain way and look like a princess. To them, looking like a princess meant not being this tall. It meant not having a figure as full as mine. My mother would watch everything I ate. I was only allowed to eat certain foods. I was forced to work out every morning and evening—more than even Claude.'

That explained why she'd eaten so little that night at the restaurant or at breakfast on the yacht. Even her refusal of anything his mother had offered.

Emilien already hated the king and queen, he didn't need a reason to hate them more, but somehow he did. He wanted to destroy them so badly. He almost wanted to set aside his meticulous plan for revenge and find a way to bring them down faster—more violently, more painfully.

'The morning of the day I left was one of the rare times my breakfast wasn't pre-made for me, and that was because a photographer was there taking pictures for a feature on us. I can't like my body and be happy with it when all I see is how I failed year after year. I can't shake those words they said to me, Emilien. I've never been able to, no matter how hard I've tried.'

He got off his lounger and sat on the edge of hers, but she continued speaking before he could say anything. As if, now that the words were flowing, their tide couldn't be stopped.

'Every single day was the same. I was told how I didn't measure up to expectations. How no man would want someone who looked like me. That morning they told me about King Héctor, they told me I should be grateful. Even now, the few relationships I've had failed because I was always waiting for them to realise that I wasn't good enough. That they'd tire of me or find someone better, and eventually they left.'

'Gisele,' Emilien said softly. As gently as he could manage. He raised her face by the chin and was glad when her brown eyes met his, but there was so much pain in them, he needed to take it away somehow. 'Your parents possess a rare brand of cruelty and even rarer lack of sense. Perhaps it was jealousy that caused them to say those things to you and treat you so badly because from where I'm sitting, princess, all I see is the most beautiful woman I've ever laid eyes on.'

'Please, Emilien. Don't...' She tried to pull away from him but he didn't let her.

'Don't what? Don't tell you the truth? The first time I walked into your shop, I was struck dumb by you. You were this perfect being surrounded by all those flowers...' He laughed at the memory. 'You were like something out of a fairy tale. Certainly not real, because real people didn't possess such perfection. When I registered your height, the first thing I thought was that you would be perfect standing beside me. Not behind me, and *definitely* not that you were freakishly tall.' She laughed and the pleasure that brought him was indescribable. 'Beside me, like the partner to my goals I had hoped you would become.'

'I can't believe the words. I've heard too many to the contrary.'

'Then will you believe evidence?' He leaned forward, pressed a kiss to her lips that sent a raging heat through his body and took her hand. 'May I?' he breathed.

She nodded once. Bracing himself against the back of her lounger, he leaned in close and drew her hand towards him, placed it on his bare chest and dragged it down, stopping over his heart, which was beating rapidly. His body was alive, nearly vibrating with anticipation. 'Can you feel that?' Again, she nodded. 'Words, princess. I always need your words.'

'Yes,' she rushed out in a breath.

'Good.' And then he kept the journey of their hands

going., further and further down, past the waistband of his shorts.

'Emilien.' His name left her lips, half-moan, half-sob.

His control was hanging on by a thread. And then he dragged her hand over his hardness and placed it there. Letting her feel him.

'This is what you do to me, Gisele. What you have always done, from the first moment I saw you.' His voice was like gravel.

'Me?' she said incredulously.

He leaned his forehead against hers, gritting his teeth. 'Yes, you.'

He couldn't think for how consumed he was by her in that moment, by the want raging in his blood. Then her touch grew curious and she began exploring on her own. She squeezed him gently and he let out an almighty moan. Desperation to have her overcame him like a fog that didn't just settle on him, but on both of them. He knew because when he kissed her, hard and bruising, she matched his intensity. Her tongue licked his lip and, when he allowed her in, she fought him for dominance in a demanding dance, proof that the fiery woman he'd wanted her to set free was with him now. The thought of going back or stopping didn't exist. He was felled by this woman who set his body on fire.

He split her kimono open and dragged his hand up her thigh. He could tell how affected she was by how frantic this kiss was becoming; by her heaving pants while their lips were still connected. He trailed his fingers down to the edge of her bikini bottoms, teasingly pulling them aside, torturing himself in the process.

'Tell me you want this.' He would need to submerge in an ice bath until he froze if she said no.

'God, yes!'

And he smiled in wicked delight.

* * *

Gisele mewled when his fingers swirled her wetness around, then threw her head back when he pushed two long digits into her.

'Emilien!' she cried out; the sound that came from him was animalistic. She opened her eyes in time to see this gorgeous, powerful man rear back and rip her bikini bottoms off her. The most modest ones she could find, the highest on the front with ruching to make her feel more comfortable.

When she'd seen Emilien walk towards her in those swim shorts, her mouth had gone dry. It had also made her want to pull the kimono tighter around her because his body was unreal. It was as if someone had taken a chisel, carved out every muscle on his torso then cast him in liquid marble. How else could she explain why he looked—and felt; she remembered his body pressed up against hers—so incredibly hard and yet touchable at the same time? His skin was perfectly unmarred apart from a tattoo. It was a quote written in typewriter script under his left pec. As he got closer, she made out the words: *Pede poena claudo.*

Latin; she wondered what it meant.

Now, it didn't matter. Now she would toss away all the clothes she hid behind if it meant Emilien would look at her like this, with fire in his green-brown eyes as his mouth lowered to her sex. She watched him kiss her passionately, his eyes fluttering closed. His pink tongue was visible with every glide of his lips. His fingers dug into her hips as if he couldn't get close enough.

Her breaths grew choppy and she looked at the sky, registering that they were outside, and back down at Emilien, who was making her feel so much pleasure, she didn't think she could handle it all. This was the single most erotic experience of her life and the thought burst through the dam of pleasure. She was trying to control it, but instead she let it wash over her, and Emilien hummed in approval.

The vibration from his voice, the sensation of his tongue and the glide of his lips, the mere fact of *him* being between her legs, all sent her climax slamming into her and she grabbed the top of the back rest, hanging on for dear life. Her chest heaving, aftershocks causing her whole body to twitch. The pleasure extended by Emilien kissing her deeply, urgently.

She had thought their previous kisses had been uncontrolled but it was nothing like this. She could taste herself on him. His every touch was hard and trembling, as if he was trying and failing to control all the passion inside him.

Her hands went to his waist band, frantically undoing the ties of his trunks, and he stepped away from her, pulling out his phone from his pocket. There was a black wallet attached to the back of it and from within it he fished out a foil square. Then he tossed the phone on the free lounger and let his shorts fall, exposing himself to her. Completely bare.

Then she watched him roll the latex on his length and her body went up in flames. 'Is everything about you impressive?' she said breathlessly, earning a dark grin.

'You're about to find out.' He clambered over her, his hand trailing lightly over her side, raising goosebumps as they went to her back and with practised ease undid the hooks of her bikini top that covered so much of her chest. 'First, this has to go.' He pulled it off her and tossed it to the side. Then he took her hands in his and held them above her head, arching her back and pushing out her chest.

'I don't want you hiding any more. You're breathtaking.' Then he closed his mouth around her nipple and it sent sparks skittering throughout her body.

She wanted more—more of his mouth, more friction. More everything. And when he dragged his teeth over her nipple that feeling only got worse.

'Emilien,' she begged and demanded. But he was unmoved. He feasted upon her, trailing ravaging kisses on every bit of exposed skin, making his way to her neck, where he sucked down, thrusting his cock into her at the same time. The sensation was so overwhelming, she shouted out his name, but no one heard her because he'd made sure they were alone.

'Fuck,' he growled.

That sound could have started a thousand fires. Maybe they had and they were all in Gisele, because she was burning with lust. Sweat formed on her skin. Her hips began rocking against him and he let her hands down, sitting back as his grip went to her hips, his eyes locked on the point where their bodies joined.

'You take me so well, princess.'

Butterflies erupted in her belly at his praise.

'More, Emilien,' she begged. Her voice came out in a whisper, even though she tried to shout.

His eyes snapped to hers, darker than she had ever seen them. With his dark hair and dark stubble, he looked like a lord of the underworld in human form. The grip around her hips tightened and he slammed his against her.

His thrusts were hard and fast, pulling moans from her that mingled with her breaths. The clapping of their skin forming a rhythmic beat. All the while he never once stopped looking at her. She was soaring, everything in her body clenching, each thrust driving her heavenwards.

'Come for me, princess.'

He slammed her body against his and she cried out, exploding around him, and then he was thrusting through her pleasure, amplifying it, until he tensed and fell forward, catching himself on his arms with a grunted curse. A bead of sweat fell from his brow and landed on her skin.

Never in her life had she felt anything so explosive.

'Fuck.' Emilien blew out a panting breath and she couldn't have said it better herself.

CHAPTER ELEVEN

THE HAZE OF lust dissipated like fog after a sunrise, clearing Gisele's mind, and she realised the enormity of what they had just done and where they'd done it. She was outside on a pool lounger underneath the bright-blue sky! Yes, they were alone on the island, but technology was a marvellous thing. Anyone could be on the water with a telephoto lens powerful enough to see them.

Emilien pushed himself off and moved towards her, but she snatched up her kimono and, like a world-class athlete, jumped off the lounger. She covered herself quickly in the kimono, holding the front closed as she rushed down the pathway towards the house.

'Princess!'

She wouldn't stop. Wouldn't look back at him. She couldn't. Who knew what might happen if she did? They'd just slept together! She'd had sex with a man she should never have been with. A man who was keeping secrets from her, who she didn't trust.

Well, not fully at least. And he certainly didn't trust her. If he did, he wouldn't have spent the better part of the week avoiding her by working constantly, telling her nothing and having only the barest conversations with her at meal times! He wanted space from her. Unfortunately, this attraction between them was chemical and so volatile that all it had taken was a little bit of kindness for it to explode. And how violently it had!

His questions had brought out her vulnerability. Not that he'd had to dig very deep, because it was always just below the surface. Being shown a little bit of care shouldn't have made her fall apart. It shouldn't have made her so needy that she fell into his arms. She was better than that.

Except, obviously she wasn't.

'Princess.' She felt Emilien's firm grip around her wrist, halting her as she reached the large, beautiful, blue and marble kitchen.

'Let me go Emilien,' she said without turning around.

'No, not until you talk to me.'

'There's nothing to talk about.'

'Really. There's nothing to talk about?' Disbelief coloured his words.

'Really,' she said, staring down at the herringbone floor.

'So what we did out there, that's not worth talking about?' There was a wild edge to his voice.

She pulled her hand from his and swung round, finding him in his shorts once more. But his chest was still bare. She almost wanted to take her kimono off and throw it at him, forcing him to cover up because she found him far too attractive. It lowered her defences against him, which was positively caveman-like of her. 'You want to talk? Fine, let's talk. That,' she said pointing towards the pool deck, 'should never have happened.'

'You're right, it shouldn't have, but it did. Do you want to tell me that you didn't enjoy that?'

'Enjoyment has nothing to do with this, Emilien. This has everything to do with us and what's going on here.' She gesticulated wildly in a way completely unbecoming of a princess, but it was the only way she could say what she needed to without succumbing to the panic building in her chest. 'You don't even really want me. This was just purely physical.'

'Are you saying I don't want you because I won't love you? What's wrong with a physical connection? I proved to you a few minutes ago that I *do* want you. I want you so damn much that I had sex with you outside when I was determined to keep my distance from you! I have wanted you from the moment I saw you. Did I lose control out there? Yes, I did!'

'And why did you lose control if you were so determined to stay away from me? You did a great job of it in the week.'

Emilien laughed but there was no mirth in it. It was pure frustration. 'You're incredible, you know that?' He ran his fingers through his hair. 'Give me patience,' he prayed. 'Gisele, I was telling you all the ways you affect me.' His voice had lowered in volume, but he was still strung tight. 'How you constantly arouse me. I was holding you and you were touching me, and forgive me if I'm human enough for my control to snap, but you wanted it too.'

He was telling the truth: she had wanted it to. She was desperate for him. He had her so aroused that she would have begged. 'I wasn't thinking clearly.' She hardly thought at all when he invaded her space. He was so powerful and overwhelming. It was hard to breathe around him, let alone think.

All she wanted to do was touch him and have him hold her against his big, strong frame. It was incredible to have him over her. She liked the way his hands felt on her body, but she wasn't allowed to. This marriage was for a year. He wasn't really her partner. He wouldn't choose to spend his life with her. He would never pick her over vengeance, just as no one else in her life had ever picked her.

'I did want it,' she said, a tad calmer, 'But I shouldn't have. I should've kept my head because we're not a normal married couple. We're only on this honeymoon so that it looks like we are. We're here so that you can play games with my parents. You're just using me, and I wouldn't even be here if you didn't need the parliamentary seat that comes with being married to me.'

Emilien's face hardened in anger. 'So I'm just using you. You're a prisoner in this marriage. You have no agency whatsoever. You had no reason to agree to this.' He took a step towards her and she took one back, just as she had done in her shop when they had first met. But she wasn't afraid of him now; she was afraid to be close to him. 'So I'm just a monster who's treated you so badly. Stole you from your quiet life in Saint-Lorin-de-la-Mer where you were hiding. I haven't offered you a means to live the way you want to…'

'I *was* living the way I wanted to.'

'You're lying!' Emilien thundered. He shut his eyes tightly and she could almost see him counting to ten. This was the perfect opportunity to walk away towards her underwater room but she should have known she wouldn't get far.

'Oh no, you don't,' he said, following her. 'You don't get to run away from me. You stand here and you fight it out.' His eyes were blazing. He clearly didn't care that she had one hand on the banister of the spiral staircase. If she went down to her room, he'd just follow her.

So instead she stayed and told him everything that was on her mind.

'Yes, I missed my siblings. And maybe to you, a man who is happy to have a big flashy house and cars and yachts, the way I live might seem like hiding. But I live to keep myself safe and so that I can make my own choices. I made my peace with seeing my siblings the way I did.'

'You mean on social media? Tell me, do you leave comments for them that they'll never see? Have they ever reached out to you?'

He might as well have driven a spike through Gisele's chest. He knew they couldn't do that, and yet he still threw it in her face. She should never have been with this man, or given herself so intimately to someone who was so comfortable using people's hearts against them. But, then again, he was far more experienced in the ways of the world than she was. Far more hardened to it than she was.

'I should never have gotten so carried away with you.' She wrapped her arms around herself, wishing, as she so often did, that she'd been born someone else, someone who wasn't so isolated from the real world. 'A man who could never love me, never care for me, but what chance did I stand with someone as experienced as you?'

'How could I love you when you're a royal?'

So he would never see her as anything more than a princess. Gisele, the person, didn't exist to him. She thought the pain she'd experienced over the years had reached a saturation point, that she couldn't contain any more. She'd been wrong.

'And experience has nothing to do with this,' he added.

'Experience has everything to do with this,' she fired back, using her outrage to keep the hurt at bay. 'If I had a little more experience than the few relationships I did have, maybe I'd be able to deal with you better. Deal with this...' she waved between their bodies '...better. Maybe with a bit more experience we wouldn't have such a lopsided power dynamic between us.'

Emilien huffed out a breath of air. 'You lack power? You're a princess, for God's sake!'

'In a kingdom where it means nothing!'

'Fine.' Emilien shrugged. 'If that's the way you want it. But, just to make things clear, you regret it? You regret sleeping with me?'

'Yes.'

Gisele wished she hadn't seen the flash of hurt in his eyes. She didn't want to hurt him but why should he be hurt? He had no feelings invested in this relationship and she needed to look out for herself. After the royal life she'd left, her sense of self-preservation was well-developed. And it told her that getting closer to Emilien was the worst possible idea, especially because there *was* good in him. The attraction was just one piece of the puzzle of why she was growing to like him. But, at the end of this, he would just walk away easily because nothing was ever real to him, while she—the woman who had wanted a partner, had wanted a real marriage and real love—would be the one who might forget herself and have hope. He'd take her heart and crush it then he'd walk away without ever knowing he had done so.

'Well, great, because I do too.' The fight had gone out of his voice. In its place there was a lifeless calm. She hated it. She reached for the metal railing to keep herself tethered to the spot so that she wouldn't be tempted to move closer to him, to bring back the spark to his voice. 'Go pack,' he instructed. 'Take what you can carry; I'll send for the rest.'

'Where are we going?' she asked in a small voice. The air was always thick when they were around each other but now the tension was different. Now it felt as though something between them had shattered. Which was ridiculous, because they'd had nothing to shatter. They were practically strangers who'd got married.

'We're leaving for Sineaux in an hour.'

'Oh,' was all she could say, gripping the railing even tighter.

'We've received an invitation from the palace.'

'I'm assuming we didn't *just* receive it.'

'No, it arrived a few days ago,' he admitted in that even tone. His voice, always a symphony, was now flat.

'You hadn't answered because you wanted to prove that you don't bow to anyone,' she guessed. 'You are playing power games.'

He didn't respond.

'Okay.' She barely hid the tremble from her voice. A summons to the palace would mean seeing her parents, her tormentors. Her siblings. She had to keep the fear at bay. She had to do this for Claude, Isabelle and herself.

She noticed Emilien's hand twitch, as if he was about to reach out but forced himself not to. He heaved a deep sigh, turned around and began walking away towards his room.

'Emilien,' she called.

'I think we've said enough, princess.'

CHAPTER TWELVE

MANSIONS TURNED INTO high-rises which turned into myriad parks as Emilien drove through the streets of Sineaux in utter silence. The only sound permeating the space around them was the hum of the tyres on the tarmac.

Gisele sat beside him, looking straight out of the wind-screen, barely blinking, moving or making any sound at all. Her fingers clutched at her skirt—an ecru and gold creation made of tweed—skin stretched tight over her knuckles. She'd never looked more royal. It was important that she did so for their visit to the palace and their first public appearance after their wedding, but that didn't mean Emilien had to like it.

He glanced at her briefly, catching a glimpse of the sunlight twinkling in the diamond-encrusted brooch on her lapel. A gryphon he had pinned on her clothes himself just before they'd left—a symbol from his family's coat of arms. Gisele might look like a royal, but he'd make sure that everyone knew that it was to a Montagne whom she was married.

They hadn't spoken since they'd left the island. There wasn't much to say. Hearing that Gisele regretted sleeping with him had been an unexpected dagger to his chest. He knew this attraction was dangerous; he knew she was a threat to his normally unwavering control.

But, when he'd heard her speak of her insecurities and why she'd had them, he couldn't not offer her comfort. However, in offering her comfort, he had to face all the reasons why he found her so alluring. The ground already disappeared beneath him whenever she was near; what chance did he stand against her when he was confessing the effect she had on him and having her touch burn over his skin?

He had shown her vulnerability. Given her proof that she could control this one aspect of him, even if it was just physical attraction. No one ever had power over him. He was stone. No one could move him, no matter what ploy they might use, so it shouldn't matter how she felt, but knowing that she regretted being with him made him want to tear at his skin.

Even though he was angry at her, and disappointed in himself, he couldn't ignore her shallow breaths or her eyes that held the same frightened, doe-like appearance they had when he'd first met her.

'Gisele,' he said. He could no longer call her 'princess'. He was putting an end to that, creating the space between them that the damned nickname was meant to preserve in the first place. But all it had done successfully was create a feeling of something intimate between them.

He'd had started calling her princess because that was what she was, a royal, but he hadn't considered what it might come to mean to him. It wasn't just the title she was owed; it was a word embodying the perfection of Gisele. A reminder to himself as to why he needed to keep his distance from her had become a reminder to both of them of who she was. Strong. Powerful. Perfect.

And not his.

Enough was enough. He would cease use of the name and end this confusing torment.

'Yes,' she responded in a small voice without looking at him. She could have been a mannequin placed in his passenger seat, for how stiff she was.

'Tell me what's going on.'

She shook her head, refusing to.

'Tell me,' he insisted. 'I can't help you if you don't tell me what's going on.' It was clear she was scared but if she could tell him what she needed he'd be able to help her through it.

And he would do so, because some of what she'd said was true. She *was* only in Sineaux because of him. Because he had gone to Saint-Lorin-de-la-Mer and presented her with this proposal that she would get to see her siblings again and he would get the parliamentary seat to bring his father's goals to fruition. While he did want to help her do that, revenge was his greatest motivator, even though he was keeping that from her.

Though he was certain she had guessed his true intentions. She was smart. It was because she was so smart that he'd made that offer, because he'd known she was likely to accept it only if she had something truly massive to gain. Emilien was extremely good at finding what motivated people and using that to get the results he wanted. He did it all the time in business, and he'd done it to her, leaving her with little choice but to say yes.

So he owed her his help. That was his responsibility to her.

'I'm afraid to go back to the palace,' she admitted. 'I'm afraid of seeing my parents. I'm really excited to see Claude and Isabelle but I'm terrified that they wouldn't care that I was there.'

'I understand that it's scary,' he replied, keeping his

eyes on the road. He couldn't look at her. If he saw the raw pain in her eyes, he would pull the car over and comfort her. 'I would never abandon you to face those people and that place on your own. I made a promise to protect you and I'm going to keep it. Sure, we don't know how Claude and Isabelle will react, but I will be by your side the entire time, and I won't let your parents disrespect you.'

'How, Emilien?' she asked, and he could hear years of exhaustion in her voice. 'They're the king and queen. They can do anything they want.'

'That's what they think, but here's something to remember: they only have power in Alouette, but you are married to a man who has power throughout the world. And, while you're married to me, use that power for yourself.' He snuck a glance at her to find her blinking back tears. 'I'm serious.'

'I know you are,' she whispered, looking down at her hands.

They arrived at the monolithic palace gates and waited for them to swing open before they glided up the driveway. Tyres crunched on gravel as they rounded a huge, ostentatious fountain.

'Over-compensating, are we?' he said, eyeing the tasteless feature. At least that elicited a small laugh from Gisele, a sound that cracked the ice around his heart each time he heard it. This time, it made him want to envelop her in bubble wrap and keep her in the car. He parked his car out the front and said, 'Wait here.'

He got out, walked around to Gisele's side, opened the door for her and offered her his hand as she stepped out, not allowing any of the doormen to get close. There was a man standing to the side in a suit holding a tablet, who instructed them to follow him.

Emilien grasped Gisele's hand tighter—a gesture that

took him right back to the last time he'd felt her skin on his—and pulled her a little closer. The proximity offered her protection because he was close enough to fend off any potential physical threats. The show of her being that close would tell everyone watching that she was important in his life, which was *his* threat to the world, should anyone think of trying anything, and, since they were linked together, there was no way they could be physically separated.

'Deep breaths,' he said softly so only she would hear, and was pleased when she obeyed.

They were led to a formal lounge with a hulking body-guard standing outside. He was only a couple of inches shorter than Emilien and dressed all in black.

Lounge was probably the wrong word to describe the room. It was a huge space with the gilded portraits of past kings on the wall to show generational wealth, power and opulence in a way that would most effectively intimidate whoever was entertained here. Just like the architecture of the palace, the interior was decorated with baroque elements—such as the purple-and-gold settee on which King Phillipe and Queen Agathe sat with sneering expressions. Claude sat on an arm chair to his father's right, Isabelle beside him. The two arm chairs opposite them stood empty, as did the love seat opposite the king and queen. And that was where Emilien led Gisele to.

Claude watched him with a scowl on his face as Gisele walked ever so slightly behind him. Emilien sat and made Gisele sit beside him. There was neither a bow nor a curtsey.

'Well, well, well, look who's back,' Agathe said, her gaze appraising Gisele. Emilien wanted to snatch her up and take her away from these people immediately. The Queen looked at his wife as if she were a bug under a microscope, making rage burn in his gut.

'Mother; Father,' Gisele greeted them.

He was proud that her voice was so steady. She looked towards her siblings, who said nothing, even though they stared back.

'I'm surprised you remember who we are,' King Phillipe said.

'I'm surprised you would show your face here again, considering how you embarrassed us with King Héctor,' Agathe added.

These people disgusted Emilien. If they thought they could say whatever they liked to Gisele in front of him, they were sorely mistaken. 'The only embarrassment was that you tried to marry off your eighteen-year-old daughter to a man old enough to be her father,' he growled.

'Oh yes, Emilien Montagne,' the Queen said, as if she'd forgotten he was there. He didn't care. She would never forget him when he was done with them. 'Our kingdom's most successful businessman.' Contempt was blatant on her face. 'I must say, I was surprised to hear that you married Gisele. We heard no whispers of a courtship.'

'Well, that's probably because you ignore the fact that you have a daughter who lives hundreds of miles away from you.'

'Perhaps,' Agathe said, unfazed. 'Perhaps it's the fact that I wouldn't imagine a man like you would find Gisele to be an appropriate wife.'

Emilien looked at Claude and Isabelle. The latter was trying her very best to hide her discomfort; the former simply said nothing, sitting there regally, doubtless waiting for his turn to rule with the same cruelty. How else could he be so unaffected by his sister's appearance after a decade, and his parents barbed words? It annoyed Emilien that Gisele was prepared to do anything to have a relationship with her brother and sister again, and yet they couldn't even be bothered to say anything or react to her. He didn't care what the King and Queen might have threatened them with; their own flesh and blood was here being treated like dirt, and they weren't standing up for her.

'You wouldn't imagine it because you have no idea what treasure looks like. Fortunately for me, I am more able to spot something with great value and exceptional rarity, so I won't sit here and listen to you disrespect *my wife*.'

Gisele's hand held onto his so tightly that there was no colour in her knuckles. Her fingernails had turned white, so he placed his other hand on top of hers to hide her show of nerves.

Except Claude noticed. Emilien saw the man's jaws grind together.

Gisele leaned closer against him. In fact, there was no longer any space between their bodies at all and, despite all the make-up on Queen Agathe's face, Emilien could see both her parents had red splotches forming on their skin.

This show of unity between Gisele and him, her hand in his, his family symbol on her clothes, was all angering them far more than he had expected. And he revelled in it.

'It's okay, *mon loup*.'

Emilien's world came to a grinding halt at the utterance of those two little words. He shouldn't like it so much when Gisele said it. He shouldn't crave to hear it all the time.

'You've never approved of my choices or of me in general,' Gisele went on, her voice growing stronger, 'But I found somewhere where I'm happy.'

It sounded as if she was talking about their marriage, but Emilien knew that she was talking about Atelier Les Jardins and Saint-Lorin-de-la-Mer. *He* didn't make her happy. Which shouldn't matter, because they would be divorced in a year, so why did it make him feel like an utter failure?

'Why should we approve of your choices?' The King's cold eyes were filled with disdain.

'Yes, why should you?' Emilien said, feeling an old anger stir alongside the new rage at his wife's treatment. 'Why should you approve of anything that's better than you when you never have before? In fact, historical evidence suggests you would just destroy it like you tried to destroy Gisele. Like you did destroy my father.'

Instantly the looks on the royal couple's faces both changed, turning threatening. Angry. Dark in a way that shouldn't be human. Gisele tensed beside him.

Isabelle seemed confused by his words and the change of tone, but Claude... Claude simply stared at Emilien, sharp green eyes trying to get the measure of him.

'I take it this isn't a subject you want aired,' Emilien said, his voice like steel. 'Given the look on your youngest daughter's face, I imagine she has no idea what I'm talking about. So would you like to resume this discussion in private?' Emilien would have liked nothing more than to air the royals' dirty laundry, but Gisele was a good person, and chances were that Isabelle was an innocent too. Out of respect for Gisele, he wouldn't be the one to shatter her younger sister's illusions about her family. He'd leave that to her siblings.

'Follow us,' the King said. His tone would have had anyone thinking they were being marched off to the gallows, but it wasn't Emilien's world that was going to end.

'Stay here and bond with your siblings, princess.' The nickname was out of his mouth before he could stop it. He wanted to catch it in the air and take it back but it was already out. 'I will be back.' Emilien got off the couch to follow the King and Queen but Claude halted him.

'Montagne, I will see you in a week. That's when you will be sworn in at parliament.'

Emilien nodded just once and made a mental note to keep an eye on the Bettencourt heir. He had the feeling Claude said little but noticed a lot.

He went through a hidden door on the wall behind the King and Queen's settee into an office that he guessed belonged to the King, given how large and exquisitely furnished it was. A view out of the window revealed the spectacular, manicured gardens the palace was known for, but he hadn't come here for the view.

'How dare you walk into our palace and throw about accusations?' The Queen seethed.

'It's not an accusation when it's true.' Emilien batted the words away as if they were nothing more than a troublesome gnat. These were rulers who had no qualms about destroying people for perceived slights. He'd heard more than one story about people having their whole worlds destroyed after not showing enough respect to the two people in front of him now.

'We want to know what you're up to, Emilien,' the King said, pointing a finger at his chest. Emilien grabbed the offending digit in a tight hold and peeled it away from his midnight-blue suit.

The king blanched. He was more than a head shorter; it would take nothing at all for Emilien to toss him across the room, but sometimes a show of power came in restraint.

'I understand my appearance in your lives must be concerning, given what happened to my father.' Emilien dropped the King's finger, pulled out a handkerchief from his pocket and wiped his hand, as if it had been muddied by the royal's touch. The king turned puce. 'It can't be easy to have your bad deeds haunt you, unsure of when the consequences might come back to bite you.' He tucked the handkerchief away once more. 'You have reason to be afraid, given the way you murdered Pierre Montagne.'

'You think we'd just let you get away with threatening us? Please, my boy, you don't know who you're dealing with.'

'Oh, I know perfectly well.'

'Let's just see what happens when we tell Gisele that you're just using her. She'll run away like the coward she is, and you can say goodbye to that parliamentary seat for whatever reason you might want it. You're never going to get it,' the King said.

Emilien walked to the table and picked up an ugly gold ornament, testing the weight of it. 'I've warned you once already not to disrespect my wife,' he said lazily. 'Consider this your second warning. Next time, I'll string you up by your entrails in front of your queen.'

He set the ornament back down and leaned against the furniture, perfectly irreverent. 'As for your threat, go right ahead. You think my wife is going to leave me, the man she married and trusted enough to return to Alouette with? I hope you're not a gambling man, Your Majesty, because I don't like your odds.'

'Whatever you're planning to do…we'll never let you get away with it,' the Queen threatened.

Emilien pushed off the desk and loomed over the King and Queen. The people who had had his father murdered and had just clearly threatened his life. 'You can try to stop me, but the Reaper is here for *you*,' he said, before walking out of the room.

CHAPTER THIRTEEN

As soon as Emilien disappeared through the door after the King and Queen, Isabelle leapt off her chair and rushed towards Gisele, who opened her arms and caught her sister, embracing her tightly.

It had been ten years but an entire decade faded to nothing in the space between them. Gisele had left behind a teenager and she'd returned to find in her place a fully grown, breathtakingly beautiful woman, but this hug didn't feel any different from the ones they shared all those years ago. All the longing, hours spent on social media and desperation—enough to marry a man she didn't know—came bursting out in a flood of tears. Tears poured down Isabelle's face too.

Gisele pulled away to get a better look at her sister. She was taller now but still much shorter than Gisele, which was a relief. At least in that one way, her mother would not have found fault with Isabelle.

'I'm so happy to see you,' Gisele said through a trembling voice.

'I missed you, Lellie.'

Gisele laughed. It was a watery sound, but to hear the nickname Isabelle had given her all those years ago, the one which had been born of her sister being unable to say her full name at first, simultaneously broke her heart and made her happier than she'd been since the day she'd left.

'I missed you too. I used to look for you every day. Both of you…' she said, glancing from Isabelle to Claude '…online just to see what you were doing and what you looked like now.'

'I hated that you were gone!' Isabelle cried. 'I don't blame you for leaving, though.'

'I'm sorry I had to go but I couldn't stay here any more. Not with—'

'Please, you don't have to explain. We were both there that morning and we'd seen what it was like up to that point. I just used to pray that, wherever you were, that you were happy.'

'I am.' Gisele nodded, crying even harder. Her sister was still every bit as caring and kind as she'd been back then. She hadn't changed, despite her parents and how cold Claude seemed. 'Are you being treated well?' If she wasn't, Gisele would be tempted to steal her away right then and she was certain that Emilien would help her do it. They'd never discussed any such thing but the feeling she had was irrefutable.

'As well as can be expected, but nothing I can't handle.'

Gisele cupped her sister's cheek, placing a kiss on her forehead just like she had back then every morning, before Isabelle went to her lessons, and every night before she fell asleep. 'I'll take you with me right now if you want me to.'

Isabelle shook her head. 'I'm safe, believe me. But tell me everything about your life. Where are you staying? What are you doing? How did you marry Emilien Montagne? I'm sure half the kingdom is in mourning!'

Gisele hadn't really considered that. Emilien was gorgeous and successful. His wealth made him famous. It seemed obvious now that he would have hordes of people dreaming about being with him. Well, they could keep dreaming.

Am I jealous?

'It's a long story.' She laughed, trying to hide the rearing of the green-eyed monster. 'I live in France now in Saint-Lorin-de-la-Mer. I'm a florist there.'

'That doesn't surprise me.' Isabel smiled. 'I still remember the bouquets you made for us when you could sneak away from Mother. Have you seen the flowers now?'

The look she gave Gisele made it clear how she felt about the monstrosity sitting on the large, round, ornate table in the room. The arrangement was a vulgar appropriation of beauty. The flowers didn't look happy; they were just expensive and the arrangement big. Just like everything else here, it was a way to show how wealthy the royals were. How much bigger and better everything they had was compared to anything anyone else could possess.

A dark house flashed in her mind, with stunning artworks and inviting couches. The palace was bright, light and golden, but Emilien's dark home held an intense beauty and warmth this place could never manage.

Because they were pieces of his soul.

She shouldn't be thinking about Emilien's inner beauty because it would weaken her heart to him, and he was off-limits to her.

Gisele scrunched her nose. 'I did. At least I don't live here,' she joked.

'So why did you come back?' Claude asked, finally saying something as he walked towards them.

The fear Gisele had confessed to in the car was real. Claude looked like the same brother she'd left—maybe with a few more lines on his face—but there was no smile, no warmth in him. She used to wonder if the brother that she'd once known would have disappeared completely and now she had her answer: he had.

'Claude!' Isabelle chastised.

'Were you happier that I was gone?' It hurt to ask the question, but his reaction hurt so much more.

When they had arrived at the palace, Emilien had taken her hand and pulled her close. While Gisele knew it had been for show, what she hadn't said to him—what she could *never* admit to him—was that she was glad to have the contact. It had felt as if she had a team mate to help her tackle her parents, something she'd never had before. He'd called her his wife, had stood up to them and promised to be by her side, but he wasn't here now, and she wished he was.

She hadn't thought she would need him to speak to her siblings, and had been grateful when he'd offered her time alone with them because this part was up to her. Reuniting with them was something only she could do. But now, face to face with Claude, she wanted to call Emilien back in. She wanted him to take her hand again. She wanted him to shield her with that big, strong, powerful body. She couldn't rely on him like that, though. She shouldn't. So she would face this herself.

'I miss you both so much. Is there no part of you, Claude, that's happy to see me or wondered where I'd been?'

But her brother said nothing. He just stood there glaring at her. Gisele stepped away and went to the window. This view of the gardens used to be so familiar to her. Once upon a time, it had been she who had sat next to Claude, where Isabelle sat today.

'When we were younger,' she said to her brother, not looking at him, 'We used to sit on those chairs, just like you and Isabelle did now, and when there was no one looking we would place our arms on the arm rests and hook our pinkie fingers together. Do you remember that?' She glanced back to see anger flicker on his face. 'Maybe you don't want to be reminded of it.' She moved her fingers over the windowsill, tracing invisible patterns. 'I still do,' she said softly.

'It will be worse than before,' he finally said, but she didn't turn round. She heard footsteps, caught movement in her periphery and realised he had come to stand next to her. A foot of space stood between them. He looked out of the window just as she did, except his hands were clasped behind his back. His spine was ramrod-straight. She could see the soldier in him, and wondered what his military service was like, but she doubted he would tell her.

'Just because you're not living in the palace doesn't mean they won't have power over you,' he warned ominously.

But the cold creep of fear was staid by her left hand being taken in a delicate hold and she found Isabelle threading their fingers together.

'Then we find a way to help Gisele.'

But Claude simply laughed at their sister. 'Always so optimistic.'

'Optimistic is better than jaded,' Gisele defended.

'You don't get it.' He turned to face her, urgency burning in his green eyes. 'Now that you're with that controlling bastard, they will see this as an attack on them. As defiance, which they won't tolerate.'

'Don't you dare talk about him like that!' Gisele's temper spiked in a way it never had towards her brother. She let go of Isabelle's hand and turned to Claude. 'What would you know about him anyway?'

'The whole world knows about his reputation, Gisele, you cannot be that blind!' he fired at her. 'The man is ruthless. No one stands against him. No one wins against him. And now he's picked a fight with the crown! Do you think there will be no casualties in warfare like that?' His eyes took on a haunted quality, but the heat hadn't left his voice. 'Our parents won't lose, but neither will he want to. Except one of them will have to.'

'Yes, one of them will have to,' Gisele agreed. 'And it will be our parents. They're evil, Claude. They have done things to his family that should never go unpunished.' Gisele thought about the way Emilien cared. The way he looked after his mother with her round-the-clock care and beautiful home, how doting he was towards her, the care he took of his company and the loyalty he showed it. Even the care he took towards her, lending her his strength today, clothing her, sheltering her somewhere he knew she'd be entirely protected.

That man deserved his chance at revenge because that need was born out of love. There was no love in this palace.

'You would side with him?' Claude asked.

'Yes!' Gisele said emphatically. She didn't even have to think about it. There was only one right side in this, and she knew it was Emilien's, despite not knowing what his revenge entailed. He still hadn't even confessed that his true motive *was* revenge.

She needed him to say it, she realised, to admit it to her. That was the only way she could ensure that, when he took her parents down, Claude and especially Isabelle would be protected from the fallout.

'Well, it certainly seems like you've picked a side,' Claude said in a softer tone. 'Just heed my warning: it's going to get ugly.'

CHAPTER FOURTEEN

G ISELE FOUND E MILIEN in the entrance hall, standing by a massive round table inspecting another garish over-sized flower arrangement. A grand stair case reached like open arms to the back of the space and several round balconies jutting out from mezzanine above decorated the corners of the room. There was plenty to look at here, but he was looking at a single black dahlia.

She'd walked into the entrance hall with her brother and sister, but it was the moment *her* foot crossed the threshold that Emilien's body came to attention and he turned around. His gaze landed on hers.

It wasn't Emilien's height that made this place feel smaller, it was his presence that made the walls close in until she could look at nothing else but him. He didn't have to hold out his hand, he didn't have to ask her to stand by him, her body simply craved to be close to his.

So she went to him. His hand came up to cup her cheek, and she noticed his brow furrow. His thumb wiped away some remnant wetness still clinging to her lashes. She re-alised then that he had been pleased to see her because, when he first looked at her, his expression had been open. He didn't smile much, though she'd learned to tell by his eyes when he would like to.

That expression was gone now. His face had hardened, his aura becoming menacing. He cast a furious glare at Claude.

'My wife wasn't in tears when I left her with you,' he growled. Gisele placed her hand on top of his and he looked back at her. 'Are you okay? Do you want me to take care of it?'

When had anyone ever grown angry because she was upset? When had anyone ever asked how they could make it better? Sure, Emilien's way of making her feel better wouldn't actually work, but the fact that he was furious because he had seen a forgotten tear created a giant crack in her defences against him.

She shook her head. 'No, I'm fine. Let's just go home.'

'As you wish.'

Gisele looked at her siblings—at Claude's cold expression; at Isabelle's beaming smile and delicate wave—saving the image to her memory. She wasn't sure how often she would get to see them in the year she would spend here, but she would remember this first visit, as well and as badly as it had gone.

Emilien placed his hand on the small of her back and she allowed him to lead her out to the car parked by the fountain in the bright sunshine. He opened the door for her and, after she was buckled in with the door closed, she looked up at the palace, happy to be leaving it, but so very sad as well. How could she not be when Isabelle's face swam in her mind? The fourteen year old sister she'd left was now twenty four. She mourned those years she hadn't got to be with her.

'Ready to go?' Emilien asked.

'Definitely.'

Emilien must have sensed that she required silence because he said nothing to her. He didn't switch on the radio, attempt to make small talk or ask how things had gone. All he did was place his hand on her thigh, his thumb rubbing back and forth on her skirt in a comforting gesture, and she had to turn away because her eyes filled with tears.

Isabelle's parting words were on a loop in her head: *We will find a way to see each other.*

Maybe Claude was right. Maybe Isabelle was too optimistic.

The thought of Claude made the tingle of anxiety in her stomach rage into a tempest that threatened to overwhelm her. His warning had been so dire, she wondered if she should tell Emilien. If she and Emilien were going to help each other, they should be honest with one other. She should tell him this. But he was keeping secrets from her too. That would end now.

They arrived at his villa and entered, and Gisele made a beeline for the kitchen, seeking something cold to drink. She didn't know how this conversation would go but at least a sip of something would ease the dryness in her throat. When she got to the large open-plan area that housed his kitchen and a twelve-person dining table, with doors that opened out to the cliffside, she found buckets upon buckets of flowers. Flowers of every kind and colour. Leaves, fillers, even the table was covered in items. Pruning shears, florist scissors, paper, tape, a selection of vases…

'What's all this?' she asked, stunned.

'I had some things delivered so that you could make as many floral arrangements as you want and place them wherever you'd like. I know it's not your shop, but I want you to be comfortable here. After all, this will be your home for the next year.'

'Emilien,' she breathed.

'I can have flowers brought in every week so you can change them out.'

Now that she knew he was comfortable with her decorating his home, she could just go to the market herself, but she didn't say it, because the fact that he was willing to do this was beyond touching.

'Thank you! I can't tell you how much this means to me.' She wanted to run to him, to hug him, kiss him, show him what words alone couldn't, but she had to stop herself because the man had who given her these flowers was still not entirely truthful.

They might not have a real marriage, but they could have friendship. They could have companionship—*if* there could just be some honesty.

He turned to leave the kitchen but she couldn't let him go.

'Emilien, wait.'

'Is there something you need, princess?'

Princess. He hadn't called her that since they'd left the island. She'd thought she hated it, but she couldn't explain the grief when he'd stopped using it and only called her Gisele. Hearing it at the palace, and again now, made her feel as if she had let out a breath she hadn't realised she was holding. And when she looked at him she saw his nostrils flare, his jaw ticking, as if calling her that had made him angry.

'I want to talk.'

'What about?'

She paced between the table and him, unsure how to start. It was probably best just to jump into it. 'You've told me that this plan was so that you could bring your father's dream, his planned legislation, to fruition, but we both know that's not the truth. I know you want revenge, and I need to know what you're planning.'

Emilien laughed, a single chuff of air. 'I had wondered if you would ask me about this.'

'So you admit it, then.'

He heaved a sigh then walked past her. She felt the brush of his shoulder and caught a whiff of his cologne as he went to the giant dining table. Pulling out a chair and spinning it round, he sat down, his thighs on either side of the back rest, his arms placed on top.

Seeing him like that, with his legs spread wide, a long column between them, his arms wrapped around it, made her think back to the lounger at the pool deck on their honeymoon, when *she* had been in his arms, and it had felt pretty bloody good. Would she feel like that again in her life? Would that be the only time that she got to experience such mind-bending pleasure?

Concentrate.

'You know, you do that a lot,' she said.

'Do what?' He frowned.

'Sigh.'

'It must be something I picked up after meeting a very stubborn princess,' he teased.

'I'll show you how stubborn I am. Talk.'

He gave her a fleeting smile before rubbing his bottom lip in thought. 'You're half-right. I *do* want to see my father's dream come to light. He was making a real difference, but I also want to get back to the place when the people rallied behind him and called for the end of the monarchy.'

'Okay,' Gisele said slowly, as she leaned against the far end of the table, turning her neck to look at him. 'And you need the parliament seat for that.'

'Yes, and only parliament can end the monarchy and move Alouette towards a democracy.'

'That all sounds very noble,' Gisele said. 'But I'm assuming your intentions aren't, or not entirely.'

'If we move to a democracy,' Emilien explained patiently, 'The nobles will have no power. I plan to turn them all into ordinary people, see generations of their work crumble and, when they are nothing and have no power, I will make them all pay for the death of my father. Your family included.'

Gisele's body exploded in goosebumps. His low threat sent a shiver down her spine. He was more than capable of making good on his threat. He was one of the richest men in the world. He *was* the richest man in Alouette.

No one stands against him. No one wins against him.

Claude's words came back to her. Her brother hadn't been good to her in years. He hadn't been kind today either, but what would happen to him? She still loved him and didn't want him hurt.

'Spit it out, princess,' Emilien ordered. 'You've come this far. Don't hide anything you want to say now.'

'I just worry about Claude. He was always meant to be king.'

'Honestly, I don't give a damn about your brother, especially not after today. He has more power than anyone seems to realise and yet he's done nothing for you apart from upset you.' There was a steely glint in his hazel eyes. He took a calming breath and glanced outside before setting his sight on her once more. 'Look, your brother is educated and rich enough to make something of his life. I'm sure he'll be fine.'

Maybe.

She turned round and began picking up flowers, absent-mindedly trimming their stems.

'You're still worried,' Emilien said.

She could feel him watching her.

'Claude might have power, but Isabelle doesn't,' Gisele said, measuring the height of the flowers in her hand against several of the vases on the table. 'What will she do? Who will she turn to? Who will keep her safe? She's an innocent in all of this, *mon loup*. I can't let anything happen to my baby sister.'

'I promise you, I will take care of Isabelle. I haven't broken my word to you yet, have I?'

'No, you haven't,' she admitted.

They lapsed into silence as the bouquet in her hand grew in size. She tested different flowers in her arrangement and adjusted the shape until she was happy.

'You really are very good at that,' Emilien said.

'It calms me. I miss Saint-Lorin-de-la-Mer and my shop. I feel like life is simpler there.' In her home, she never worried about protection or revenge or political schemes. She didn't worry about losing her heart to a man who would never love her but kept doing thoughtful gestures, such as buying an entire shop's worth of flowers. He was a man who was so soft on the inside, but piercing that thick armour around him was impossible. No one would ever get through. Back home, she lived quietly and worked peacefully.

She heard the sound of Emilien's expensive shoes on the hardwood floor, and the next thing she knew his body was brushing her shoulder as he leaned over her, picking up a rose that he twirled in his fingers.

'This rose is beautiful, princess, but it's been cut off from its life source. It's dying. Will it still be beautiful when it's dead?'

Maybe he was right. Maybe she was barely living, but she wasn't the only one. 'The same could be said for you. You've cut off what gives you joy to focus only on the practical.'

And, for the first time since she had met him, Emilien gave her no response. He simply placed the flower back on the table and walked out of the kitchen, stopping only to look at a painting. His painting.

Gisele put down the flowers in her hand and picked up the rose he had just discarded. The blood-red petals were only just opening. This was her favourite stage of a rose, when it reminded her of a champagne flute. She clipped the stem much shorter than all the others, picked up the book on the corner of the table that she had been reading out on the terrace that morning, placed the rose within the book, pressing it between the pages, and put the book back where she had found it.

A heat on the back of her neck made her glance round and she saw Emilien still standing there, watching her with an indecipherable look on his face. Without another word, he walked away.

CHAPTER FIFTEEN

EMILIEN SAT BEHIND a large wooden desk in his midnight office. Light streamed in from behind him, shining across the space, landing on the tan Chesterfield sofa on the opposite side of the room. His silhouette carved a penumbral doppelganger on the leather. He stared at the sofa, lacing his fingers under his chin, propping his elbows upon his sturdy desk. Everything was coming together.

It was almost three months since he'd married Gisele, since she'd moved into his home, and the evidence was everywhere. Such as the vase of flowers that had replaced the brass globe on the console table behind the sofa. Like their wedding flowers, the ones here were always a mix of dark and bright.

After that day when they had returned from the palace to all the flowers he'd had brought in for her, she'd asked him if she could place a bouquet in here and what he would like. She'd asked him every week since and his answer was always the same: he wanted this one, a mix of both of them. Except today Gisele had added a new touch. Instead of the baby's breath, waxflowers or spray berries she usually used, she'd added little red gems that sparkled as the light caught them, reminding him of pomegranate rubies.

Having reminders of her in every nook and cranny of

his home made it impossible to escape the attraction to her that seemed only to grow day by day. It was torture, being so close but never kissing her, or taking her on every surface in the villa, like he so badly wanted to do. He didn't understand how Gisele was able to cope when he thought about her nightly and spilled himself in his hands with her name on his lips.

But still, he was growing to love her presence, to love sharing every meal with her. Even when he was away on business he had to take her with him. The terms of the parliamentary seat were clear—spend an entire year together. Impractical for almost any couple, it was a deliberate means of maintaining control over who got to rule the country. But Emilien wasn't just anyone, and he needed to keep this seat.

When they did have to travel, he took her to one of his many resorts, and called her regularly during the day, telling himself it was to ensure she was safe, but the truth was he wanted to hear her voice. When they were at the villa, she made the place come alive. Even when she was locked away, working on the management of her shop and having video calls with her team, he still felt her presence in the house.

He looked forward to dinner every day, when she would tell him about Isabelle, who was being protected by the world's most dedicated bodyguard; she spoke to her almost daily on the secure mobile phone he had given her. Or she would tell him about the great idea she had had for her business, or some desire she had always had but could never satisfy. Every night, she asked him about his day, and it felt good to confide in her. He liked answering her questions about his life. He liked taking her to his resorts and giving her a taste of the opulence she had been missing. Because of her, every day there was just little more laughter within his walls, a little less loneliness and a whole lot more longing.

And with each daily interaction that chemical desire flared brighter. The need to touch her grew and he kept finding reasons to do so. He'd put his hand on the small of her back to guide her. He'd tuck an errant lock of hair while she worked, or brush away imaginary smudges on her face.

And, every time he did, she leaned into his touch. Her pupils flaring wide.

They were still drowning in this attraction, but Emilien wouldn't let them go back to that place where she regretted being with him. Not that she'd given him any signal that she wanted to have a taste of him again.

Despite not wanting to get close to a royal, three months of having her in his home had led him to some place he didn't have a name for. Not friendship, not a relationship, but something that felt deeper than either and yet not quite enough. But the fact that she'd been here three months already meant that in nine she would be gone. That was the agreement they'd made and she'd given no indication that she might want to stay longer than that.

Why would she? Once the year was over, she'd have everything he promised her. She was already speaking to Isabelle at least once a week. He had made it possible for the two of them to meet in secret locations a handful of times but, once he took the monarchy down, there'd be nothing stopping them from resuming a normal sibling relationship.

Her brother had kept his distance, a fact Emilien knew hurt her. If it wasn't for her begging him not to hurt Claude, he'd destroy the prince alongside her parents.

And their destruction was coming along nicely.

Emilien had already sat in several sessions of parliament and was starting to see the fruits of his labour. Industry listened to him. The changes he wanted to make to business in the kingdom had long been in place in his own companies so he could prove without argument that they worked. That increasing workers' wages and benefits would not drastically impact profits because, when he'd showed good faith to the unions, they'd reciprocated and had been more willing to negotiate and make concessions. And with the size of profits businesses were reporting—his included— the difference was a marginal percentage. Emilien had approached the captains of industry almost sympathetically. He knew they had shareholders to appease, he had his own, and that made them willing to listen to him.

He hoped that, if his father could see him, he would be proud. But the man was dead and there was no way to know.

The press was having a field day, comparing him to his father, and the name Pierre Montagne had almost rekindled a sense of revolution in the people of Alouette. Emilien had just read several articles about his proposed changes. Most praised the benefits; a few had labelled him a harbinger of doom. He knew it was because those media outlets were loyal to the monarchy and dismissed their opinion. Still, he instructed his PR team to get on that immediately. But what pleased him the most was the number of people speaking out against the royal family. Questioning what they did for the people. Questioning what made them worthy rulers, loudly wishing for new ones. Emilien had tossed a little ball of snow down the side of a mountain and it was quickly turning into an avalanche.

'That's quite the smile on your face, Mr Montagne.' Gisele stood at the French doors that led into his study, her hands held behind her back, her shoulder leaning against the door frame.

Good Lord, this woman was beautiful. Glossy brown

locks curled slightly over her shoulders, stopping at her full breasts. She wore a bright summer dress today. Not a garment from the wardrobe he had provided her with. He had given her clothes to fit her new role. Not just as his wife but as the returning princess. Clothes that would give her confidence and negate any scrutiny of her appearance. That anyone would take issue with her looks was inconceivable to him, but the world was cruel.

In his home, however, he was exceptionally glad that she wore the clothes that she had chosen for herself. A reflection of her personality. She felt safe enough to be herself around him, and that was a privilege.

He tried to picture this place without her and his frozen heart cracked.

'Maybe I was thinking of you, princess.' She would never know how often he did.

'Such a flirt,' she teased. 'And I would never presume to think a smile like that could be because of me. More like you read the news.'

She was truly blind to how she affected him, and he should have been disturbed that she now knew him well enough to guess correctly at what he'd been doing, but he couldn't find it in himself to be.

'Are you just going to hover at the door or are you going to come inside?' He pulled off his glasses, tossing them on the table.

Come inside. Sit on my lap. Let me touch you.

She bit the inside of her cheek, uncertainty flittering on her face, which only made him more curious as to why she was here.

'Come in here or I'm coming out there,' he said.

'So bossy.' She rolled her eyes as she walked up to his

table and brought out from behind her a sketch pad and a large box of oil pastels.

Mixed media medium grain paper, he read on the cover as she placed both down on the table in front of him.

'Flowers bring me happiness, Emilien, and art does the same for you. I see the way you look at the pictures on the walls, see the way you look at your own. You miss it, don't you?'

He wanted to deny it but what use would that be when she could so clearly see the truth? He couldn't insult her intelligence like that.

'I do, but I don't have the time for it. This life I live, princess, it requires sacrifice.'

'I don't doubt that, but if you keep sacrificing pieces of yourself and the things you love, what will you have left?'

The answer was a successful company, happy employees and lots of money and power.

'But you will have lost yourself. Don't give me that look, Emilien; your answer was practically written on your face.'

He laughed—something he seemed to do with increasing frequency around her—and pulled the sketch pad towards him, revealing the first blank page. He ran his fingers over the white surface. How long had it been since he'd touched one of these? He didn't even have art supplies any more.

'I don't have time,' he said, yet he could see an infinite number of possible drawings dance on the surface.

'*Mon loup*, it is a Saturday. The markets are closed. The politicians are probably out on their yachts, so you can take the afternoon off.'

She wasn't wrong.

'What do you want me to draw?'

'The question isn't what I want you to draw,' she said, admiring a frame holding a painting of the very first yacht

Talaria had manufactured after he had taken over. Emilien had painted that himself. A photograph would have been easier and quicker, but there was satisfaction in slowly creating a piece to appreciate the hard work he had put into making the subject of the artwork.

'The question,' she continued, 'is what would make *you* happy to draw? What makes you happy, Emilien?' she asked, bracing her palms on his table and leaning towards him.

What made him happy?

Such a simple question with such a complicated answer. He wasn't sure any more. He couldn't remember when he had last been truly happy. He supposed revenge made him happy. *Satisfaction.* His success made him happy. *Pride.* Seeing his mother taken care of made him happy, because he could do all those things for her. *Fulfilment.* None of those things were exactly the same as being happy.

He glanced down at the paper and then back up again, catching a glimpse of those flowers. Maybe the answer was in front of him. Quite literally leaning over his desk.

One day soon that light would move out of his house and, as beautiful as this place was, the black walls would become oppressive. It could be a reminder that, for a little while, he didn't mind the floral fragrance that now permeated his halls.

'May I draw you?'

'You want to draw me?' Gisele asked as if the request was completely absurd. 'Why would you draw me?'

'Why wouldn't I draw you?' he deflected. 'You bought me this very thoughtful gift. It would be the height of bad manners if I didn't use it to show some gratitude.'

'And you're nothing if not a well-mannered gentleman.' She laughed.

He should record that sound so he could play it back when she was gone.

'Okay,' she allowed. 'What should I do?'

She could do anything, and she would be the most spectacular thing he'd ever drawn.

'Lie on the sofa,' he said.

She took off her sandals and propped her feet up on the leather, leaning her torso against the curved arm rest like the subject of a renaissance painting. She already looked so perfect there.

He had hoped that her constant presence would help him develop some immunity to her, but that hadn't happened at all. Instead, every day was torment, because every day he just wanted her more, but he couldn't go back there. Not since the last time they'd slept together and she'd regretted it afterwards.

He steeled himself for the way her touch made him feel and went over to her, adjusting her posture and angling her face so the sunlight caught her brown eyes in a way that made it hard to breathe. It made him want to threaten anyone who looked at her with bodily harm, to keep them away, so that he alone could witness their magic.

'Comfortable?' he asked.

'Yeah.'

'Good.' He pulled out a pencil from his desk drawer and rolled his chair around his desk, placing it diagonally to the sofa so that the sun was cast on Gisele without any interference from him. Then he sat down and quickly began sketching an outline.

Asking her to be the subject of this oil-pastel painting was probably a stroke of genius because now he got to admire her, study her every curve for as long as he wanted. He got to torment himself with his need to touch her, and give her pleasure without touching her at all, apart from the caress of his eyes. Every inch of her was perfect right down to her toes.

Gisele let out a heavy breath.

'What's wrong, princess?' he laughed, having a clue about what she might say.

'I like the idea of being drawn, but it's quite boring just lying here.'

'I knew you were going to say that.' He was pleased he'd guessed right. 'So, talk to me.'

'Will it not distract you?'

He halted the movements of the pencil across the paper to cast a withering glare at her that once again made her laugh. Today was a good day. He'd managed to pull two of them from her.

'Okay,' Gisele said. 'How did you learn to draw so well? Did you take lessons?'

'No. It was just something I used to enjoy as a child, and after my father died and my mother left Sineaux I was left with huge amounts of time to stew in my anger. My grand-father bought me some supplies and told me to draw it out.'

'Draw what out—your grief?' Gisele asked incredu-lously.

'The best way I can explain it is that it takes time. It's almost meditative. You get the feelings out and it gives you some clarity. When we came back from the palace,' Emil-ien said as he tossed his pencil onto the table and opened the box of pastels, pulling out a colour and starting to fill in the image he'd sketched out. 'You were upset at how your visit had gone. You were upset at me. You were wor-ried about Isabelle and Claude and so you started putting flowers together into a bouquet.'

'It calmed me,' she said softly.

Emilien caught her eye and gave her a smile.

'I understand,' she said. 'But for the last few years you haven't done any of this. All you've done is work, take care of your mother and scheme.'

'Like I said before, sacrifices have to be made.'

'I know I'm only going to be your wife for a few months longer, and then you may never want to see me again, but can I ask you for something? A favour?'

'You can ask me anything.'

'Don't sacrifice yourself, please.'

'I think it's too late for that.' He had given up far too much. He had come way too far to take his foot off the gas when it came to his vengeance. When it came to realising his goals and all his other responsibilities. It didn't leave time for frivolity, so he did the only thing he could think of and lied.

'I promise, princess.'

She would never know whether he'd kept his word once she was gone, when he was alone once more.

He shaded in the picture, using his fingers to smooth out the strokes of the oil pastel. His fingers worked on the paper with the same worshipping touch he craved to use on her body. Layer after layer, and colour after colour, Gisele came to life on the sketch pad exactly the way he saw her: like a goddess. And finally, when he was done, he closed the box of pastels, his fingers smudged and dirty, and tossed them on his table with a rattle that jarred Gisele from the relaxed state she had fallen into.

'All done,' he announced.

'Can I see it?'

'Of course.' He got off his chair and handed her the

sketch pad. He was a man who never cared what anyone thought. Opinions weren't facts and they didn't concern him.

Yet, here he was, hoping she liked this drawing. Why did it feel as if he was handing her his heart?

CHAPTER SIXTEEN

GISELE ACCEPTED THE drawing from him.

'Emilien!' she gasped. 'This is incredible!' She looked up to find vulnerability in his eyes that, when she blinked again, was gone. Hidden.

'I'll be right back,' he said and walked out of the study, leaving her alone with the picture. She so rarely came into the study and only once had she ever come in here alone. Emilien had left early for a meeting and she had taken the opportunity to snoop through his computer and save all the files he had compiled on her family and her onto her phone. At the time, she'd thought it was a smart way to protect herself from all sides. But now, looking at this picture, she knew she didn't have to protect herself from Emilien.

She'd never seen herself like this. The creature in this picture was breathtaking and the artist who had drawn her... Well, he clearly felt something for her. There was so much emotion in the artwork, just like in all his pieces. And yet there was something different about this one. This picture took her breath away and saddened her at the same time. Why did she get a sense of longing from the image?

It couldn't be Emilien's longing. He was a good man, but he'd already admitted he could never love or care for her in the way she wanted. Even though she didn't want the title, she was a princess, and having royal blood was a hurdle he could never get past. Not to mention the fact that he was so closed up. He would never entertain the vulnerability of love. He had told her as much.

And, if all that wasn't reason enough that Emilien would not be longing for her, then there was the fact that their marriage would come to an end in nine months, and he had said nothing about wanting her beyond that, despite how easy it was to live with him. Their daily talks had made her feel as if things were slowly changing between them, that he was allowing her to know him. But despite them growing closer, and despite the attraction that still burned between them, he hadn't given her a single clue that he wanted anything beyond their year. And he was a man who went after what he wanted.

Still, she couldn't get over the emotion in the picture because the man who'd drawn it clearly had some kind of love in his heart.

Emilien wasn't unfeeling. Maybe he didn't care about her in a romantic way, but he did care. He cared about a lot of things. So much, in fact, that he had taken up his father's cause as the way to exact his revenge for his death.

Why, though?

He had so much money and power he could get away with doing whatever he liked. So why this?

'Can I ask you a question?' she said, as soon as Emilien re-entered the room.

'Another one, you mean.' He smirked but he must have seen something on her face that made him drop the expression and gave her his full attention. 'Of course.'

'Why did you choose to fight the same fight as your father? I mean, if revenge was all you were after, you would have found a different way. I feel like there's more to this.'

Emilien took a deep breath then went to the window, looking out at the choppy sea. He clasped his hands behind his back and she could still see a few dots of colour from the oil pastels around his nail. Those smudges brought warmth to her heart, and made her breath catch in her throat, because Emilien was always so pristine, so perfectly put together, and he'd deliberately sullied himself. Tainted his perfection because she'd asked him to draw her a picture.

'Because of my father's friend, a man of no importance to the kingdom. Just an ordinary person with an ordinary job, taking care of his family,' he started, and she paid close attention, ignoring her feelings.

'He and my father were close friends since they were children and I had grown close to him too. He was a proud man. There was a huge gap in wealth between our families but he would never accept any assistance from my father. He always said all he wanted was a friend to share a wine with. A few years before my father was killed, his friend's wife became ill and they didn't have the means to pay for her treatments, so my father stepped in and for the first time his friend accepted the help.'

Emilien rubbed his eyes with his thumb and forefinger. He looked so tired, exhausted in a way no human should ever be. Gisele wanted to go to him but she stayed exactly where she was. She remained so very still because he was talking and she felt that this was an important piece of him to collect.

'Despite all the treatment, his wife died anyway, and the funeral was expensive. My father's friend refused help with that. He only wanted to save his wife. Unfortunately, with the expense of the funeral and losing her income, the family hurt badly. He had to sell his home, move somewhere a little further away, somewhere smaller. Their lives became uncomfortable. It wasn't enough that they'd been through this tragedy, but they had to live the consequences of it every day afterwards. My father vowed to make a difference after that. He started negotiating between parliament and corporations, on behalf of the unions, for better wages and benefits, and that was the beginning of the end for him.'

He turned round, resting his back against the window and crossing his arms over his chest. 'My father didn't want to watch people like his friend suffer, and that's why I have foundations in place to help people in the way he would have wanted, but it's not enough. The *system* is rotten, Gisele, and people like your parents and their sycophants benefit from it. It's time it changed, and I can't let my father's death be in vain. It wasn't just Pierre Montagne that we lost. It was the mother I used to know too. She left for two years and, when she came back, she wasn't the same. Have you seen what depression does to a person? I have.'

Gisele felt a tear land on the hand that still held the sketch book. She wasn't just crying for what Emilien, his friends and family had been through, but also because finally she had the full picture of his heart. She could see clearly beyond his high walls, beyond the armour, to a man who was simultaneously dangerous and loving, single-minded and good, and she loved his heart.

She loved him. She knew he couldn't love her. She could never change her blood. He would never allow something like love into his life. Something that could make him weak.

All the reasons why they couldn't be together stacked up in the space between the sofa and the window. They were huge cement barricades, things that couldn't be moved, but she loved him beyond all those barriers.

Given the look on his face and the picture in her hands, he might feel something for her too, but it wasn't love.

Whatever it was, it would never be enough for Emilien to choose her over revenge. He needed that revenge and that meant he was still only with Gisele until the parliamentary seat became permanent—nine months. They were so completely temporary.

More tears fell down her cheeks. She placed the artwork of herself on the sofa and walked towards him, a slave to this feeling in her heart. Every barrier between them broke her bones just a little bit more until she reached him, emboldened with this strength of what she felt for him, and quivering with the pain of harbouring this unrequited love.

She placed her hand on his cheek, his stubble scratching her fingertips, her eyes locked on his. He leaned into her touch, not just a little bit this time, but fully angling his head towards her hand. Scraping the rough surface of his cheek against her palm. Seeking more.

'Princess,' he mouthed soundlessly and yet it was the loudest thing he'd ever said to her. The nickname had once been an annoyance. She hadn't liked it because she hadn't wanted reminders about who she wasn't good enough to be. She hadn't liked how that name was a way for Emilien to keep her away and remind them both of why they could never have anything more, but she'd made her peace with him saying it.

But now, with softness in his eyes and what he had just confided in her, it felt like the most intimate thing. He was so open to her for once and she leaned up and brushed her lips against his. She heard as much as felt his breath falter. She pulled away, searching his face for any sign that he might not want this, but there was none and so she kissed him again, deeper this time. There was no hesitation from Emilien as his arms banded around her body, pulling her as close as he could. Her free hand was on his chest, over his heart, and what had started as a slow and steady thump was now racing.

She'd kissed him before but all those times it had felt like a magnificent, otherworldly attraction. Those kisses had been a culmination of all the physical things they'd felt. It was true she hadn't felt anything like those before but, compared to this kiss, they felt superficial.

Into this kiss she poured all her longing and her love. She could taste the months of restraint on his tongue, feel it in the slide of his lips against hers, in the way his teeth scraped only lightly against her lips, nowhere near as hard or urgently. He was trying his best not to let this go to that place where everything became physical and rushed. Burning. Without thought. It made her guess that, just like her, he was trying to remember every nibble, glide and taste.

She opened her eyes as he broke the connection of their lips, his forehead connected with hers. Just moments before, she'd felt his control slipping, and now there was a pained look on his face.

'Princess, we can't do this.'

'Why not?' she breathed. How many more 'princesses' did they have left? She wanted to tuck away each one he gave her, hoard them in her heart.

'Because the last time we did this, you regretted being with me. I can't live through that again.'

His words scraped her raw. Over the time she'd spent with him, Gisele had come to realise just how important it was to Emilien always to be strong, never to show any weakness or vulnerability, but he showed it to her right then.

'Things are different this time,' she said. It wasn't the act of being with Emilien that she regretted, because she would replay that passion in her head over and over; it was the fear of losing herself to him that had made her put up barriers. But now that fear made no difference, because the battle was lost. Her heart was Emilien's even though his wouldn't be hers. 'Things are changing,' she added. 'I want to, Emilien, but if you don't want me, I understand.'

She stood still as he took her face in his hands, the touch beseeching her to understand what he was about to say. And, with his warm touch and his hazel eyes so close, the study fell away, the ground fell away. They weren't in Alouette any more. They weren't even on earth. He transported them to a place where only they existed and nothing else. It was him and her, and none of the trauma from their pasts or the evil of the people in their lives. It was just them.

'These months have been torture,' Emilien said. 'Every day I smell you in my home. I eat my meals with you. I see your flowers brighten up my dark walls, and every moment of every day I want to pull you to me. I want to kiss you and pleasure you. I want to place the world in the palm of your hands and tell you to rule over it, over me. I never stopped wanting you, Gisele. Not even once.'

Did that mean things were changing for him too?

'Take me, Emilien. Show me.'

He kissed her gently, reverently. He picked her up, holding her against his chest and her arms wrapped around his neck. She wondered if he would take her to his table, maybe the sofa, but instead he walked out of the French doors and down his gallery hallways. Up, up, up they went, his eyes never leaving hers as he traversed the steps that led to his room.

And what a room it was. She hadn't been in here. It was the one place she hadn't asked to place any flowers because she had no reason to enter. Yet, the first thing she saw as he put her down was a small, narrow vase with only a few blooms inexpertly cut. The thorns were still on the roses. There were no filler leaves or the little flowers she used to make soft transitions. These were a few flowers stolen from her supply and brought up here, placed on the small table between his over-large bed and the accordion glass doors that opened onto a large balcony.

Darkness and light intertwined in that vase, nearly black and luscious pink. The stems were cut a little too long. They were uneven in the vase. A black flower stood a little taller than the pink ones.

Just like the two of them, she thought.

'Take me now, Emilien.'

CHAPTER SEVENTEEN

'Undress me, princess,' he said, taking a deep breath when her fingers went to his charcoal shirt, unbuttoning it in a touch that blazed. She pushed it off his shoulders and it slipped down to the floor.

He had to bunch his hands into fists when she undid his jeans. When she peeled off his layers, it felt as if she was removing his armour, piece by piece. The soft swish of fabric was a loud clang of metal to him, but he did nothing to stop her.

He wanted this. And, when she stripped him down to his bare skin, he moved closer to her. Kissed her hard with a deep, inhaling breath as if somehow that could make this kiss live inside him. As if it could brand her into his soul.

But she already had been. Not just because of the way this day had gone, with her bringing art into his life again for however short a time—not just because he'd seen her heart break when he'd told her of the events that had led them down this path of revolution and revenge—but simply because she was Gisele. A single bright spot in his dark world.

He slid the straps of her dress over her shoulders, seeing all the moments they'd shared with new eyes: the way she had affected him from that first meeting, to him wanting to protect her, to being hurt that she regretted being with him; the way he loved it when she called him *mon loup*.

Mon...

He liked being hers.

And he certainly was her wolf. He would be a sentry by her side as long as she wanted him to be. He would protect her with a viciousness the world was yet to see.

Her dress fell to the floor with a crash as the truth shattered over him. The reason he dreaded the end of their arrangement, the reason he'd brought her flowers into his bedroom, was because he loved her. He didn't know when it had happened, or how it had done so when he'd rejected the idea of it, but he loved her.

Emilien had never wanted the vulnerability of love. He didn't want to give himself to someone like that and hurt the way his mother did. He didn't want to do that to anyone else either, but the reality was that it had never been a choice. It had never been a choice to care about someone like this. Never been a choice to let them in. They'd let themselves in. It had simply happened, and not even power like his had been able to stop it from happening.

His feelings were proof, because he'd fallen in love with the one person he would never have chosen. A princess.

'My princess,' he whispered, kissing the juncture where her neck met her shoulder as he removed her bra from her body. The sound she made brought him to his knees, and he met the carpet willingly. The man who never bowed, never knelt. Not to royalty, not even in the church he used to take his mother to all those years ago. But he knelt before Gisele.

He pulled down her panties with tantalising slowness and looking up to capture her gaze, placing his mouth over her heat.

'Emilien!' she cried out, her fingers diving into his hair.

With her tight grip and her taste on his tongue, Emilien was overcome.

How much longer will I have you? The thought pierced his newly exposed heart.

The need to hear her come apart was more urgent than ever, so he gripped her hips as he licked and sucked, listening to her breath get choppier; her moans, louder. And then he placed her leg over his shoulder, getting deeper with his tongue, and she came apart spectacularly. Instinctively, he wrapped his arms around her back, steadying her as her orgasm almost shook her off her feet.

But he wasn't done with her yet. He needed more.

Her eyes were closed and her chest was heaving but Emilien was already back up, taking her face in his hands and kissing her with the might of his love. He walked her backwards until the backs of her knees hit the bed.

He could have taken her in his study, could have laid her over the chesterfield and had his way with her, but it hadn't felt right. He wanted her in his bed. He wanted the sunlight on her skin and the sound of the ocean to carry them away. He wanted to smell her on his sheets and hold her while they slept.

'Tell me what you're thinking,' Gisele said, out of breath. She had one hand on his side, the fingertips of the other skimming over his tattoo. 'What does this mean?'

He didn't want to tell her—he didn't want to remind her of his thirst for revenge and give her a reason to leave—because a man like him didn't deserve a rose. He was only meant for the thorns.

He swallowed, praying she wouldn't run from him, before in a low, gruff voice, he said, '"Punishment comes limping".' His fingers, embedded in her hair, lightly scraped against her scalp, back and forth, making her eyes flutter closed. Was he calming her? Offering her comfort? Or was this a nervous tic? It wasn't something he had ever experienced before. 'It's Horace.'

She nodded wordlessly.

'And I'm thinking that I desperately want to be inside you right now. I need you more than air, but in a feeling that's completely foreign to me. I'm afraid to.'

That was only half the truth. The other half was that he wondered what it might take to make her stay. They were already living together. Why couldn't it be like this every day?

Because she didn't tell you she wanted to stay. She wants freedom. And you're about to destroy her family. Because you will leave her, or she will leave you, and then what? Everything ends. Someone has to become a shell.

Just like his mother, barely functioning without his father. Emilien was a lot of things, but he wasn't cruel enough to inflict that kind of hurt on Gisele, who had already suffered enough. And he wasn't masochistic enough to put his heart through a shredder like that.

'Why are you afraid?'

'Because, even though you said you wouldn't, you might run.'

'I won't. I promised.'

He watched her as she looked to the side, then opened his bedside drawer and pulled out a foil square.

'How did you know they were there?' he asked, not caring if she knew because she had been snooping.

She smiled. 'I guessed. The position of everything here is so considered; it wouldn't make sense for these to be anywhere else.'

His breath died when she ripped it open and slid the

latex along his length, then took his hand and gracefully climbed up on the bed, making him follow her.

'I promised,' she repeated, then lay on her back, head on his pillows, and tugged on his arm. 'These smell like you.'

'Then I should change them,' he said. 'So that they only smell of you.'

Whatever she'd been going to say didn't make it past her lips.

'You look so perfect in my bed, princess.'

'It would *feel* perfect if you were next to me.'

Emilien took one more look at her then lay on his side next to her, placing one arm under her neck. With his free hand, he guided her thigh over his hip. He didn't know how many more days like this he had left with her, but today was special. Today she'd broken him and made him realise he loved, her even if she would never do the same, so he wanted to see every expression on her face as he took her. Feel her breath ghost over his skin. Touch her in every conceivable way.

He took his cock in his hand and held it at her entrance. His body begged him to thrust into her, but he couldn't yet.

'I need to hear it,' he pleaded. 'Call me *yours*.'

'*Mon loup*.' Her voice broke on that second word, and it was all it took for him to sink into her, feeling exposed, like a live wire. He thrust into her slowly, languidly, as he kissed her, the same way. Taking his time. Nibbling at the feast that was Gisele's pleasure. His fingers sinking into her every full curve. Her body rocking against his in perfect harmony and he was taken back to that first day when he'd wondered at how perfectly she would fit against him. The answer was: utterly.

She was the missing puzzle piece that fit against his oddly cut corners, the day to his night. But the truth was that, if he was the captain of his yacht, she was the horizon—magnificent and all-consuming. He would chase it for all his days and never reach it, because she was his only for now.

The thought had him burying his head in her neck, his arms tightening around her.

'Let me see you, Emilien, please,' she breathed around a moan that made her sound needy. 'I need more.'

'Me too, princess.' But he knew she meant more pleasure, whereas he meant more of her. His thrusts grew hard and rapid, pulling from him groans that matched her song of passion.

'Give me your hand,' he instructed. And, when she did, he placed her fingers in his mouth, his tongue licking each digit.

'Fuck,' she moaned.

Chuckling, he brought his lips to her ear has he placed her fingers where their bodies joined, moving her hand in firm circles.

'That's not very princessly of you,' he teased. 'But who cares when you're so fucking perfect?'

'Emilien,' she whined. Her voice high pitched. Her body as tense as his as they barrelled towards release together. His body growing ever warmer. The string in his spine pulled ever tauter. Rising higher and higher. A moment of light-headed euphoria that might have been a blink of an eye or an eternity, and then with a grunt from him and a keening wail from her that sounded a lot like his name, they were in freefall. Her slick heat pulsing around him just as he did into her, fuelling each other's ecstasy. Bodies intermeshed. Skin slick. Breaths heavy. He was holding onto her as tightly as she gripped him. Coming down together back into themselves.

And then he kissed her. He kissed until her breathing returned to normal and until she was panting again. He kissed her until she was ready for another round, and kissed her afterwards until she grew drowsy.

And, when she was limp in his arms, he whispered one solemn word into her ear that he knew she would never hear. 'Stay.'

CHAPTER EIGHTEEN

GISELE WOKE TO the sight of Emilien's muscular back rippling against the backdrop of the Sinelaise cliffs and coastline. He pulled on a pair of black jeans and shrugged on his discarded shirt from the day before. They hadn't left the bed since Emilien had carried her up here, not even taking a break for sustenance, and Gisele's stomach chose that moment to protest very loudly.

Emilien's shoulders shook with suppressed laughter. 'Good morning, princess.' He leaned over her to place a small kiss to her lips that she wasn't ready to end, so she fisted his hair and kissed him harder.

Her heart was bruised from her realisation the day before—that she loved him—but she wouldn't have changed a thing about what happened afterwards because bliss coloured with a little pain was still bliss.

'Where are you going?' she asked when he pulled away.

'Unfortunately, we cannot survive on a diet of sex alone, so I might forage some breakfast.'

'In the wilds of your well-stocked refrigerator?' she teased.

'It's very dangerous. You never know what wild animal might be hiding behind the door.' It was a privilege getting to see Emilien like this—fun, a little carefree. She might even have said happy.

She laughed. 'Oh, I know.'

Emilien's eyes darkened. 'That animal is always ready to make a reappearance for you, princess.'

She was just about to make a snappy retort when her phone buzzed. She had no memory of bringing it up. Obviously Emilien had done so after she'd fallen asleep. The texts she received while in Alouette were mostly from her shop and Isabelle, so she automatically reached for it and opened her messages.

She felt the blood drain from her face. All levity from moments before was lost.

'What's wrong?' Emilien asked from the foot of the bed.

'It's Isabelle,' she replied.

'What did she say?'

Gisele appreciated the urgency in his tone. It was as if fun Emilien had been instantly locked away, replaced by the dominant man who ruled the world.

She swallowed hard and read the text aloud. "'I'm being moved to the Azure Palace. I think they're going to take my phone. Not sure when I will be able to contact you. I'll try to find a way!'" The Azure Palace was at the edge of the city. It was more private and secluded than the main palace—not as grand but far more beautiful. It was where her grandparents had lived after they had stepped down from the throne for her parents to rule, but no one had stayed there in years as far as Gisele knew. Her parents were doing this to keep Isabelle away from her.

Would they find a way to keep Claude away too? She hadn't really seen him since their reunion. He wasn't as enthusiastic about her as Isabelle was, but right now there was still the possibility she could see him. Her parents could take that possibility away.

'Don't worry, princess, I'll fix this,' Emilien said. He and the bedroom re-materialised as he pulled her from her rapidly growing panic.

'How?' she asked, looking at the phone screen while holding the dark sheets tighter to her body. 'How will you fix this, Emilien? You can stop Isabelle from being taken today, but what about tomorrow? Or the next day? What about Claude? You know what this is, right? It's retaliation against you!' She scrunched her fingers in her hair. 'I'm being punished for being married to you.'

'Princess, we had a plan.'

'Yes, we did, and our plan involved you getting a parliamentary seat to change the labour laws in this kingdom and me getting my siblings back. That was your offer at the restaurant in Saint-Lorin-de-la-Mer, but so far I've had a taste of what it might be like to have a relationship with them only to lose them again, and I *can't* lose them again!'

'Just trust me to find a solution, Gisele.' There was a frustrated edge to his voice but she couldn't take heed of it right now.

'From where I'm standing, the solution is simple. You already have support to change the laws. If that's all you want, then maybe they'll back off, but they know you want revenge. Please, can't you find another way?' she begged.

Emilien reared back. 'You cannot be asking me that.'

'Please, Emilien, I'm desperate. Is destroying them going to bring anyone back? Is it going to fix anything?'

'It's justice,' he said harshly and began pacing his large bedroom. 'You have no idea how long I've been planning this. I've come too far, sacrificed too much, to give up now. I can't give this up for you. For anyone.'

The panic in Gisele's heart ratcheted higher. She was afraid he was too lost to his need for revenge to see any other way, so maybe it was up to her to do something. Isabelle had no power. Gisele had virtually none, but maybe… maybe if she parted from Emilien, her parents would stop focusing on her and she would be able to see Isabelle again. Even if Claude wanted to have nothing to do with her, the possibility to see him would once again be alive.

But parting from Emilien would mean losing everything she had with him: the chemistry, fun and love, however one-sided. The very thought of walking away from him was a slice right through her soul. It was pain beyond anything she'd endured before, and she had been hurt more than most people could comprehend. She loved her husband. She didn't want to lose him before she was forced to, before their agreement terminated.

And yet what choice did she have? She was forced to choose between her siblings and the man she loved. A man she'd had for a very temporary amount of time, a man who wouldn't love her back. But her siblings were her family for life. A decade apart hadn't dimmed her love for them.

And what if Emilien were the one fielding this choice— would he choose her? Of course not. He'd already told her he would never choose her over what was important to him. He hadn't even picked her for who she was; he'd picked her for what she could give him, a seat in parliament. She could have been anyone. No one chose her, they only ever wanted to use her, so she had to be true to her own goals… and therefore she had one choice.

She placed her phone on the bedside table, only just noticing a book sitting there.

That's where it went. She had last seen it the day they had returned from the palace, so she picked it up and out fell the flattened rose. The rose Emilien had touched. She wanted to save it, hold onto it, but she shouldn't have. She touched the bud and a petal fell free. Dried and wrinkled. Dead.

Throwing the covers off her, she got out of Emilien's bed, leaving the scent of him behind, and forced down a sob, knowing she would never experience it again but having no time to savour it one last time. She looked around for the pieces of clothing he had stripped from her body when it had felt like he was making love to her.

Foolish thought. He'll never love you.

If she focused on just getting dressed, maybe she could keep the tears at bay. Maybe she could keep her soul together just a little bit longer so she could walk out of this house in one piece, because the only way she would get her end of the deal was by leaving the man she loved.

Every thought was written on Gisele's face. Emilien watched as she pondered her options, trying his best to remain calm, but things were changing here. He just needed her to realise that her best chance was with him.

Come on, princess. Please don't do what I think you're thinking.

She tossed the covers off and started getting dressed. He knew then she was coming to the wrong decision. And, once she slipped her dress over her head and fixed it in place, she looked at him. In that expression he saw everything he didn't want to.

'You can't leave,' he said lowly. His body was frozen as dread smothered all his short-lived happiness. Anger rushed to fill the spaces between every cell in his body.

She couldn't leave. He needed her for his plans. If she

left now, he would lose his seat and all the work he'd done; the momentum he'd gained would be gone.

Is that the only reason she can't leave? a voice in his head asked, demanding him to be honest with himself.

'Gisele, look at me.' 'I love you,' was on the tip of his tongue but he couldn't make the words fall. Not when he'd decided long ago that he would make himself invulnerable to the weakness of it. When he'd told her that he would never love her.

Maybe he should say it, though. Maybe he should say anything to keep her here.

'You promised that I would always have a choice.' Her voice shook, eyes swimming with tears. Seeing her hurt like this crushed his heart into sand and, when a tear kissed her cheek as it fell, his body unlocked and he went to her, brushing the wetness away with his thumb, but she didn't lean into his touch. She stood still, staring into his eyes.

'You do have a choice, but I can't let my plans fall through. Not for anything, Gisele. I thought you understood that.'

She closed her eyes, twin streams cascading down her cheeks. 'I'm such a fool,' she whispered brokenly. 'I thought things were changing between us.'

'Things are changing,' Emilien said forcefully, his hands on her shoulders imploring her to listen. 'They *have* changed.'

'Show me how!' she yelled. Her eyes widened at her own outburst.

He huffed a disbelieving laugh. 'Is that the first time you raised your voice to someone?' Despite his dread, panic and anger, a tendril of pride wove its way through him. The shock on her face transformed into a blazing fire in those brown eyes. To him, it seemed as if a cast that had been moulded over her, that had restricted her and had hardened in place over time, had shattered into a million pieces, revealing who she was always meant to have been. Revealing the woman he knew had been in there all along: someone who was brave enough to make difficult decisions; someone who was brave enough to defy everyone; someone who was able to start a new life. She had strength and he was getting to witness her realise it.

'Do I have my siblings in my life? No,' she said with an eerie calm. 'They've been taken away again. Do I have any sort of freedom? No, because I'm in Alouette and married to you, and according to you I shouldn't leave until your plans come to fruition. In fact, I'm worse off than before you appeared in my life, because I don't even have my independence here.'

He saw her spy the vase with the mismatched flowers. His terrible attempt at an arrangement had had only one purpose—to bring her in here in some way.

'I left everything behind and came here because I trusted you. I must have, otherwise I would never have got on that yacht with you, would I?'

'But you won't trust me now.' And it hurt.

'How can I, Emilien? I've been nothing but a pawn in your game all along.'

He stumbled, as if he had been slapped. 'That's what you think?'

'That's what I know. I was one to my parents, and I am one to you. Sacrifice the pawn and have the best position to take the king and queen.'

'Please, Gisele, I can't do this without you.' He didn't want to, and for more reasons than just the power she gave him in the kingdom. He grabbed her chin and forced her to look at him. 'I don't want you to leave.'

But all she did was place a hand on his and pull it away from her chin, turning his blood to ice in the fraction of time it took her to step away from him.

'All I wanted was freedom and safety, and some family, and I'm getting none of that. I'm sure you'll find a way to make your plans work but it'll be without me.'

Then she walked out.

'Princess!' he called, racing after her through the house towards the front door. She'd already pulled it open. 'Wait!' he commanded. 'What will it take to make you stay? We can figure out this thing with Isabelle together.'

Giscle slowly turned around, standing on the threshold. 'Tell me that things have changed. Tell me that there is something more between us. That this isn't just about revenge.'

Emilien's spine stiffened. She wanted him to admit his feelings. Without a doubt, things had changed for him, and all it would take for her to stay would be for him to admit the truth he already knew in his heart—that he loved her—but she had no idea what that admission would cost. Images of his mother at her very worst flashed through his mind. When Emilien had been a fifteen-year-old taking care of his parent and not the other way round.

What if he said the words and she left anyway because all she'd wanted from this arrangement would be hers? Because he *would* push through with his plans, taking revenge and thereby allowing her to reunite with her siblings without fear for any of them. Or what if he said the words and she too was taken from him the way his father had been taken from his mother and him? Life always took things away from him: his father, the mother he'd known before his father's death, his grandfather. He never wanted the vulnerability of love. He never wanted this pain, which would only be a fraction of what would await him down the line.

The words to make her stay were right there but he just couldn't bring himself to say them. Especially when she hadn't said them either.

'You knew what this marriage was meant to be,' was the reply he gave her robotically and, God, did it eviscerate him.

Gisele exhaled a slow, sad breath. 'Goodbye, Emilien.'

Then she turned around and walked away. He was powerless to stop her as she took his love, and his parliamentary seat, with her.

CHAPTER NINETEEN

A LUXURY BLACK sedan pulled up to where Gisele stood. It was fancier than the one Gisele had booked but, with her heart shattered and her mind overcome with thoughts of Emilien and Isabelle, she didn't question it. The company had probably recognised her name and wanted to put their best foot forward for the wife of the kingdom's most powerful businessman. *Soon to be ex-wife.*

A man in a suit opened the back door and she gratefully climbed inside, unable even to mutter a thank you. If she opened her mouth all that would come out would be the sobs she was holding back with fracturing walls.

The windows were tinted dark, and she was thankful for the privacy. As the driver shut the door, she thought his suit didn't fit anything like Emilien's did. The image of her husband in his preferred three-piece black suit popping up in her mind and the pain that lanced through her in response stole her breath.

Do not think about him.

She couldn't if she was to survive this trip.

She was heading to the airport where she would catch the first flight back to France. Once she was home, she would let her parents know that she had left Emilien, that she posed no risk to Isabelle or to the crown. She had to firmly establish that she was no longer with her husband before she attempted to contact Isabelle, for her sister's safety. If she went to Isabelle first, her parents could retaliate in an unpredictable way, thinking she was acting on Emilien's will.

Without her, Emilien's threat would be neutralised and that would have to stand as proof that she wasn't against her family. It was the only way to have contact with her sister and, once she had that, she would let herself fall apart. Mourn the loss of Emilien from her life. Cradle the love she had for him in her heart, knowing she would never see him again. There would be no reason to.

And, once she stitched herself back together, she would send for her things and start the divorce proceedings.

She stared out of the window, saying a quiet goodbye to the streets she'd called home for the last three months. She watched wordlessly as they navigated the road that led to the airport. But…

This wasn't the way to the airport.

Gisele hadn't lived in Alouette in a decade but she still knew her way around. They should have left the motorway two exits ago. In her anguish, her heartbeat had turned to sludge, but now it was growing faster and faster, like a hummingbird's wings.

Don't panic.

She remembered Emilien's words. *You are married to a man who has power throughout the world. And, while you're married to me, use that power for yourself.*

'Where are you taking me?' She injected as much haughty confidence into her voice as she could, hoping she sounded like a woman who was Emilien's equal. But the driver didn't answer. Instead, she heard the snap of the doors locking and the whir of the privacy screen going up.

No. No. No. This can't be happening. Think, Gisele! She looked at her phone. She'd just said goodbye to Emilien, but if she was in trouble he would help, wouldn't he? She had to try. With shaking hands, she unlocked the device to find she had absolutely no signal. How was that even possible? 'Breathe,' she instructed herself. Locked doors didn't mean they stayed locked. They were moving at speed but an injury from throwing herself out the car was better than whatever hell awaited her at the end of this.

She pulled on the latch twice to unlock it, except the door wouldn't budge. Child lock. There was no way to get out unless she broke the glass, but if it was bulletproof that would never work. Then the car took an exit, and the road sign she saw through the window told her exactly where they were going and who had intercepted her car.

The royal family had a safe house an hour outside Sineaux. It was meant for emergencies and was never used. Emilien wouldn't know about it. No one would, apart from the security that worked for the family. Once this place had been used, it would be sold and another would be found.

Gisele sat back in her seat, stomach churning, sweat breaking over her brow. *Dear lord, what is waiting for me over there?*

Eventually, they pulled up at a villa that looked ordinary enough, except Gisele knew it would be made of reinforced concrete and intruder-proof glass with shutters that could roll down in an instant.

'Come on,' the driver said, as if he hadn't just kidnapped her.

He marched her into the house, the door slamming closed behind her, and walked her into the lounge, where her mother waited on a settee with four guards next to her.

'Gisele,' Queen Agathe greeted her.

'Mother.' Gisele was terrified. She towered over her mother but, in her head, Agathe had always been an insurmountable figure. 'What are you doing?'

The queen clicked her fingers and the guards surrounded Gisele. Her phone was snatched away by one of them who linked arms with her, forcefully taking her to a room and shoving her inside. Then they parted like the sea as Agathe stepped forward.

'Why are you doing this?' Gisele demanded.

'Because Emilien Montagne needs to re-learn a lesson, and to do that we've taken away what he treasures most. You see, while you were with Emilien it was impossible to reach you. The best I could do with you being so protected was tap into your phone.'

'What? How?' Gisele's blood ran cold.

'I've had Isabelle's phone cloned for a long time. I couldn't risk her turning into a rebellious let-down like you, so I always needed to know what she was up to. Access to her phone gave me your number and tapping into it was as easy as sending you a text from what you thought was your sister.'

Gisele tried to remember every conversation she'd had with her sister, hoping they hadn't said anything that would endanger Isabelle. What about her calls with Emilien? Had they ever spoken about his plans on a call? She couldn't remember!

'It was simple,' Agathe sneered. 'Who's going to say no to your father and me?'

'Emilien,' Gisele replied. 'And you wanted to separate us.'

'My daughters are terribly predictable. The moment I took Isabelle away from you, you panicked and left Emilien long enough that we could swoop in and take you away from him for good.'

'Just like you took his father from him.'

The smile on her mother's face was nothing short of evil. Unfortunately for Gisele, the Queen was wrong. Gisele wasn't the thing Emilien treasured most, revenge was. He had just chosen revenge over her, so her mother's plan wasn't going to work. Even so, she was enraged at what her parents had done to her husband. What they were trying to do now.

'How could you kill his father like that?' Her voice shook with anger she had no ability to control.

Her mother tutted. 'You never had what it took to be a royal. You're my only failure, Gisele.'

'Thank you,' she ground out.

'Sacrifices have to be made to maintain power,' the Queen continued.

Gisele thought of the things Emilien had told her, how he'd sacrificed pieces of himself. What had her parents ever given up? 'None of it has ever been your sacrifice,' she fired at her mother.

'No one said it had to be.' With a smirk, her mother rose, turned round and walked out.

Just as Gisele flew towards the door, it shut with a heavy thud, locking her away from Isabelle, from Claude…from Emilien.

Emilien sat in the arm chair in the corner of his bedroom, his back to the view. The tan leather was warming as the early afternoon rays beat down on him. The cool ocean breeze gave some relief from the oppressive summer heat.

But maybe it wasn't the summer heat that had him burning. Maybe he was just in hell.

He'd held the rose that had been pressed in Gisele's book, gently twirling it in his fingers, for the past few hours. He had wasted the entire morning sitting here. There was work that needed doing, for his company, for his plans, but he couldn't do it. Couldn't care about it. Not when Gisele had left and torn his heart out of his chest.

Hollow.

He was just hollow.

It was funny. He had bemoaned their attraction. He'd wished to be immune from its potency, from its distraction, but if he thought Gisele's presence was distracting, it was nothing compared to her absence. Every shallow, emotionless breath reminded him of her. Felt as if he'd inhaled corrosive acid that was slowly dissolving him. His only thoughts were of her. His memories were of her. The feeling of her in his arms. The euphoria of her lips on his. Where was she now? Had she already found a flight back home?

Home. Saint-Lorin-de-la-Mer wasn't her home, this was. Here with him. But she was gone and in her place there was only silence.

How could a person be numb and still feel as if they were being hacked into pieces?

Because you love her...but what choice did you give her?

Should he feel guilty? Did he have anything to feel guilty about?

Staring at the pressed flower, Emilien thought hard about what it had been like from the start.

He'd known Gisele before she'd had any idea of him. Known he would marry her solely for what she could give him and had given her no choice in the matter. Even though she'd said yes, he'd said exactly what he'd needed to get to that yes just as he would in a business negotiation. Except Gisele wasn't an acquisition, she was a person with feelings, fears and desires, and he'd used that against her. He'd used her desperation against her. If he'd been forced to keep away from his mother and father, he would have been desperate too. Especially if that separation had come about when he'd just been a teenager.

And then, when she had married him and made as little fuss as possible, he'd told her he would never love or care for her. A blatant lie, because he'd chosen a private honeymoon so that she would have time to get used to being back in Alouette. He'd wanted to keep her from the eyes of the palace until she was ready. He'd slept with her because he wanted her. He'd comforted her because her pain was his.

But he had taken her away from her comfort and safety, from her shop. He'd said *trust me* and she had.

He should feel guilty because he'd done all of that just to have revenge in the most satisfying way. He could have simply exposed the King and Queen; he had the proof. He could have formed an alliance with someone already in parliament and made sure to receive invitations to negotiations. He'd done none of that.

I've been nothing but a pawn in your game all along.

He couldn't blame Gisele for thinking that.

God, he loved her so much. Why had he been he so blind to how he felt?

'*I wish I died with him. I still want to.*'

'*Mama, you don't mean that.*'

'*I do, mon fils.*'

'*It's been two years.*'

'*It will always be too soon for me.*'

A wet spot landed on Emilien's charcoal shirt jarring him from his stupor, and when he touched his fingers to his cheek, they came away damp. No one would ever understand how close he'd come to losing both his parents.

No one knew that his grandfather giving him Talaria hadn't just been to ensure that the legacy of the company lived on through him, but also that Emilien would have something to keep him together if his mother did die.

He had been blind because he was protecting himself from love. How could he want to love when he'd seen that? When he still witnessed his mother's complicated grief every time he saw her?

But there was no protection against loving Gisele. She'd barrelled through his defences. She'd brought colour to his monochrome world. She'd brought light, laughter and smiles. She'd shared with him what brought her joy. The proof was twirling in his fingers.

'I don't want to live without you,' he said to the flower. The words scared him, for how close they sounded to his mother's.

Sometimes I'll open a book and find a rose pressed amongst the pages. Other times a daisy...it makes me feel like he's still with us.

Gisele had done the same thing but this flower was in Emilien's book. Was this a reminder she had planned *for* him or was she being hopeful for a future *with* him? Did *she* want to find it pressed in the pages years from now?

He wanted that more than his next breath—for her to still be with him.

There's only one way for that to happen.

He needed to give up this need for revenge. Isabelle was a complication. With the King and Queen controlling her, there was no way Gisele could be with him. All she wanted was to have a relationship with her siblings and all Emilien wanted, he was coming to realise, was Gisele.

The choice came down to Gisele or revenge. His heart or his goals.

But wasn't he making that choice right now? Gisele had left and he was a shell of a man. Sitting here, he didn't care about revenge. He didn't work or check on his plans. He just wanted the love of his life back.

'I need you,' he said to the flower. 'I'd do anything to have you back.'

Anything? Even choose Gisele over revenge?

And he knew then that he would. He wanted revenge for his father, a man who'd been so full of love that he had taken on an entire kingdom for the people he cared about. That man wouldn't have wanted this. Maybe he could let go of his vengeful plans. Maybe instead he would only seek to change the labour laws because his thirst for vengeance wasn't worth losing Gisele. Or their love. Love was what had set him down this path but his love for his father couldn't cost him the love of his soul mate.

She wouldn't be taken away from him the way his father had been because he could protect her from anything. Maybe love would make him vulnerable to Gisele, but loving her would make them both invulnerable to everything else, because Emilien would never let any threat touch them again. He had power, and he would use it for them.

'I'm going to get you back, princess.'

Sound and colour returned. The haze lifted. The first thing he needed to do was find out where she was. She'd already been gone hours. It was entirely possible she was already back in France.

Emilien sprang out of the chair and fished out of his pocket the phone that he had been ignoring all day. He called Gisele but it just rang until he went to voicemail. Maybe she was flying.

If he got on his private jet right now, he could reach France soon after she did. But a voice at the back of his mind told him that he needed to give her a choice this time. He was prepared to fight for her, and he had to start somewhere, so he sent a text.

Tell me where you are, princess. Talk to me or I will be at your door in an hour.

He discarded the wrinkled shirt he wore but, before he could reach for a clean one, a message flashed across the screen of his phone.

It was from Gisele. His heart, which had all but stopped beating for hours, launched into a sprint. At least she was responding to him. But, when he opened the message, his stomach sank.

I've gone back to the palace. Don't come looking for me.

Alarm bells went off in his head.

'This doesn't make sense,' he said to himself, his voice scratchy. 'She'd never go there.' He knew her. Maybe she wouldn't want to see him after he had hurt her but, with how she'd been feeling when she'd left, the only place she would have gone to was Saint-Lorin-de-la-Mer, where she felt safe. She would have proved to her parents that she had left and tried to reach Isabelle in the least confronting way to keep her sister safe.

Something was wrong.

'I'm coming, princess.'

Emilien pulled on a clean shirt as he ran down to his garage, barely pausing to snatch a set of keys before he was in his fastest car and racing to the palace. He would find answers there.

* * *

His tyres skidded to a stop, kicking up gravel, and before they had even settled back on the ground he was out of the car and running up the steps to the palace doors.

They already stood open, as if they were expecting him. The same man he had met before came rushing towards him holding a clipboard.

'You have no appointment with Their Majesties,' he said irately, but his aggravation was no match for Emilien's rage.

'Take me to them right now,' he growled.

The man stepped back with a nod. 'Follow me.'

King Phillipe and Queen Agathe sat upon the same settee they had occupied when they had first received Gisele and Emilien, looking royal and unconcerned.

Emilien's vision turned red.

'Where is my wife?' he growled.

'Lost her, have you?' the King sneered. 'Have you tried looking for her?'

'I'm giving you one chance to tell me,' Emilien said. 'We both know she won't stay lost to me.'

'Big, scary, Emilien Montagne…' The Queen laughed. 'You'll never find her.'

'You overestimate your abilities,' Emilien replied. 'And underestimate mine.'

'You think we can't make Gisele disappear?' The Queen curled her lip. 'Let me be clear, Emilien, the only way you will ever see Gisele again is by agreeing to drop this vendetta against us. Pull your proposals and forget about revenge.'

He'd already given up the idea of revenge but his proposal to change the law…that he couldn't let go of. That would help so many people. He would just have to find

Gisele on his own. 'I will raze the world to the ground to find her and then—'

'And then what?' the King questioned. 'You'll come after us? Given what you're certain we're guilty of, do you really want to take that chance?'

How dared they? How dared they threaten the woman he loved? Emilien's blood turned to ice. He couldn't risk Gisele. He loved her too much. All he wanted was her back safely.

'You want me to give up my revenge for Gisele? Fine— done. Because, unlike you, I know how precious she is, but you can go to hell if you think I'm going to let the people of this kingdom continue to suffer.'

'Well, then, I think that hell is the only place that *you* will meet Gisele,' Queen Agathe said. Judging by her expression, she thought she had won.

Maybe she had, because Emilien would never do anything that further risked Gisele's life or wellbeing. He wanted better lives for the people of the kingdom, but he wanted Gisele more. He *loved* her.

And, forced to choose between the people and Gisele… hc chose Gisele.

'You would hurt your own daughter?' The disbelief should be alien, considering all that they had done in the past, but he had hoped that maybe there was a line when it came to their own flesh and blood. Clearly, he'd been too generous.

'We would protect the monarchy,' the Queen answered.

Emilien walked up to the back of the seat that he and Gisele had once sat on and gripped the gilded back rest so tightly that the wood creaked. 'No, you wouldn't. If you hurt my wife, you will ensure your demise and the absolute destruction of the monarchy. You hurt my wife, and not even the devil would stand against me when I come for you.'

A pallor crept into the King's skin and it satisfied Emilien to see that he knew exactly what fate awaited the Queen and him if anything happened to Gisele. But he couldn't revel in the King's fear, because his wife's safety depended on him, so he turned around and stormed out.

CHAPTER TWENTY

GISELE STOOD AT the only window in her room. She lifted a hand and knocked on the glass. The sound was thudding and heavy. Unbreakable. She'd known it would be but she had to try anyway.

She'd been locked in here hours already, with no means of communication: no television, no radio, no books. Just the silence and her thoughts for company. She had no idea who was on the property, or how many guards had remained behind, because of course there would be a few.

When the door had slammed shut on her, the panic of being locked away, the pain of leaving Emilien, the anger at her parents' plan had all overwhelmed her, and she had slid down the door, unable to stem the guttural sobs that escaped her through huge fissures in her soul. She didn't know how long it was before the tears had finally dried and she started looking for any way out.

But there was none to be found. So here she was, staring out of the window at the patch of green grass and the trees beyond, wishing it were the cliffs of Sineaux that overlooked sparkling waters as far as the eye could see—a view from a dark house owned by an even darker man with love in his heart and revenge in his soul.

She missed Emilien so much. Craved his presence and

comforting, seductive scent. Where was he? In his home, forwarding his grand plans to bring down her parents? She had to admit, she now wanted him to succeed. Or was he in his office working? Aboard his yacht, maybe? Was he half as devastated as she was for leaving?

'You probably don't even know where I am,' she said, her breath ghosting over the glass. 'And you can never come here. It's too dangerous.' She turned her back on the disappointing scenery and sat on the floor with her back to the bed, hugging her legs. Unless she spontaneously developed super-powers that would allow her to escape, there was nothing left for her to do but wait.

And wait she did until her limbs went numb. Until she heard movement outside the door.

'Hello!' she yelled scrambling forward. 'Is someone there? Please! Help me!'

Instead, of an answer, an envelope was slipped through the crack beneath, thick and eggshell in colour. When she picked it up, she found that it contained something heavy and solid.

She ripped it open and her phone fell out but there was one more thing in there: a letter. She unfolded the page and read:

Hang in there. Emilien is looking for you. He's coming, Gisele.

He came to the palace to find you because they sent a spoofed text. The king and queen threatened you if he didn't drop his vendetta against them. He chose you.

Just be patient. You'll be free soon.

Gisele's heart was racing. Her eyes darting back to that one phrase. *He chose you.*

Who'd sent this letter? Who was looking out for her? The writing was so familiar. In fact, she had seen it before: ten years before, on the note that had made her escape possible...

But she had seen it more recently than that. If Gisele hadn't already been sitting, the realisation would have knocked her feet out from under her. The memory of a visit with Isabelle, when her sister had pulled out a note from her bag.

'Look, Claude wrote it down for me...'

This was Claude's handwriting.

'All this time,' she breathed. 'All this time you had been helping me.' Quietly, from the shadows, because he had to take the throne. He couldn't jeopardise that, and who knew what her parents would have done if they'd found him assisting her escape?

She was overcome with guilt as she saw his reaction to her return in a whole new light.

'So why did you come back?'

He hadn't been unhappy to see her, he'd been concerned that she had returned to more torment. His warning had been to protect her.

'Oh, Claude,' she whispered. 'I'm so sorry for ever doubting you.'

It was criminal that her brother was forced to hide his concern because of their deranged parents. It was abominable that they were using her against Emilien. Enough was enough.

Gisele unlocked her phone and went to her files that could only be opened with facial recognition. She'd saved all the evidence Emilien had collected as insurance for her own safety, but it was time it was used for its intended purpose. Her parents had got away with enough and, with Emilien having apparently chosen her over his revenge—a fact she couldn't quite digest yet—it was up to her to make things right.

Having taken away Gisele's phone, her parents had clearly thought there was no need to interfere with the signal in the safehouse. She sent the files to every news agency she could find the contact details of. Then she took screenshots and posted to her social media accounts, the accounts that she had once used to keep an eye on her siblings anonymously. Accounts that used to be private but which she now made public. The time for being anonymous was over. She wanted her parents to know it was her—their disappointing daughter—who'd brought about their demise.

Emilien had just thrown open the door of his car when his phone buzzed. He fished it out of his pocket, got inside and closed the door before checking it.

To his surprise, the number belonged to Claude.

The message contained a series of numbers that were obviously co-ordinates, a code and an instruction:

...two guards on the property. Hurry.

'Thank you, Your Highness,' Emilien whispered. The prince had just saved him an enormous amount of time trying to track Gisele down. He raced towards the gates that only just opened enough to let his car out before he was flying through them.

Speed laws simply didn't exist as he followed the GPS directions, his heart racing in his chest. His stomach was in knots. His anxiety grew with every moment it took to get to his wife.

'Hold on, princess.' He sent up a silent prayer that she would be okay, begging that he would find her unharmed. And then a ping diverted his attention to the screen in his car that displayed the dynamic map.

A wide band at the top read:

Breaking: Evidence leaked of King and Queen's guilt in Pierre Montagne assassination.

'Gisele,' he breathed. But how had she managed to do that? 'It doesn't matter,' he told himself, his eyes flicking back to the road. What mattered was the strength it had taken her to do so and he found that he wasn't upset that she'd taken his vengeance from him. He was just proud of her for taking a stand.

A second ping followed shortly after.

Breaking, it read once again, *Crown Prince leading the charge for the apprehension of King and Queen.*

Strangely, Emilien didn't feel disappointed that he wasn't the one making them pay. It just felt as if an oppressive weight he'd forgotten he had been carrying had lifted off him. It was funny; Gisele was the one who'd wanted freedom, and yet, she had found a way to free him.

He needed her in his arms. He needed to show her what she meant to him. He needed to tell her he loved her.

A quick glance at the map showed he was nearly there. 'I'm coming, princess.'

CHAPTER TWENTY-ONE

THE DOOR TO the room flung open with a bang.

Gisele spun around, electrified with shock and fear, only to find Emilien standing in the doorway. The top of his hair just about brushed the doorframe.

A beat passed between them. Two beats. And then his long strides ate up the distance between them and, before she could register what was happening, she was engulfed in his arms.

'Emilien?' she whispered, unable to believe he was there.

'I'm here. I've got you.'

Her wish to be held by him, to have his comforting scent envelop her, had come true and she was overcome. Overcome with relief and worry and anger and sorrow and everything else she'd felt that day. It came pouring out in a torrent of tears that she had no means to stop.

'Shh,' he comforted her while she clutched onto his shirt, unable to let go. 'I'm not going anywhere, princess.'

She'd thought she was all cried out, but it seemed as if there was another dam that needed bursting within her. Emilien didn't complain that she was making a mess of his shirt, he just held her tightly. He made her feel protected, cherished. He held her until her tears finally dried. But she still didn't want to step away because, when she did, they would have to talk.

Claude had said Emilien had chosen her over revenge, and it was hard to believe, but here he was. That didn't mean that things had changed. It didn't mean that he was ready to love but it seemed as if he was giving her no choice because he pulled away, holding her at arm's length.

'Are you okay?' he asked, his gaze scanning every inch of her.

'I'm fine. They didn't hurt me.'

'They'll still pay,' he growled.

'I told you, I'm fine.' She should step away but, when his hands cradled her face, there was no way she could do that.

'But you might not have been.' He touched his forehead to hers. 'God, princess, I have never been that scared. I only had clues to know if you were okay. All I did know was that you were alive.'

'Clues?' Gisele asked.

'You released the information about my father's murder.'

Of course he had seen that.

'How?' he asked, still attached to her. Bending like this could not be comfortable for his tall frame but he made no move to stand back up, to create space. 'Why?'

'Claude found a way to give me my phone after my mother took it away. I had snooped on your computer months ago and saved the files on my phone.'

He looked at her then, eyes wide with surprise. 'You'd have needed my log-in details.'

She smiled. 'I think you were too used to living alone, because your computer had your credentials saved.'

He laughed softly. 'Of course.'

'I just couldn't let my parents get away with murder—quite literally—any more.' Gisele looked around the bland room in which she had been locked away. Who knew how long they'd intended to keep her here? She would have lost what little freedom she did have in her life.

She had no idea where the pieces were falling now, where she stood with Emilien. She broke out of his embrace, taking a few steps away. 'I'm sorry for destroying your revenge plans. You're probably upset that I took it away from you.'

'I don't care,' he said gruffly. 'Gisele, I'm the one who's sorry.'

'You are?'

She watched him run his fingers through his hair and finally took a good look at him. Dishevelled hair. Jeans, the same jeans he'd worn the day before. A different dark shirt. The bottom button was undone, as if he'd missed it in his haste. He wasn't the perfectly put-together man who had come to her store.

'I lost sight of what's important. What matters most. And that's you, Gisele.' She saw remorse in his hazel eyes, pain. Love. But she was afraid to believe it. 'You're more important to me than anything else in the world. Your love means more to me than any revenge or money or power. And nothing matters without you in my life.' He threw his hands up in the air. 'Do you know what I did after you left?'

She shook her head. She had imagined him going about his day as usual. Maybe that hadn't been fair, because he was hurting right in front of her.

'Nothing. I couldn't do anything. I was paralysed without you. The house reminds me of you. The flowers, the scents…it's all you. Everything good in this world comes from you. I sat in that chair in our bedroom for hours, unable to move because nothing mattered any more. Not without you.'

'Emilien, I...' she cried.

'Love me? I know you do, and I was careless with your heart. Forgive me, princess.'

'I already did, when Claude told me you chose me over revenge. My parents threatened me.'

Emilien nodded. 'I had already chosen you before I went to the palace. You walked out, and I had to think about what was truly important to me, and that's you. Only you and so, when I confronted your parents, they threatened you if I didn't let go of it all...revenge, the labour proposal...and I chose you, Gisele. I would choose you again.'

Gisele couldn't form words over the tears filling her eyes and the lump in her throat. She knew what changing the laws meant to him. *Why* it was important to him.

'I'm sorry.'

'Don't be. I love you. Only you. I can live without everything else but not without you,' he said as he stepped towards her. 'Why didn't you call me after you got your phone back?'

'I figured there were a few guards on the property and I couldn't risk your life by bringing you here.'

It seemed that Emilien had reached the end of his patience, because he drew her into his arms and hugged her once more. She heard him inhale her scent, mutter to himself, 'Safe,' as if he needed to convince himself of that fact one more time. 'They've been taken care of,' he said eventually. 'I wouldn't be standing here if they weren't.'

'Are they dead?' she asked, afraid of the answer.

'No.' He laughed. 'But they are bound and gagged. A gift for your brother.'

The nightmare was over, then.

'Are you ready to go home?' Emilien asked.

Gisele didn't know how to answer. Yes, she was...but where was home?

* * *

Emilien felt her try to pull away. He didn't want to let go, because contact with her was the only thing that calmed him down, but he did. He had been more scared than he could ever remember after getting the text that obviously hadn't come from her, but seeing her unhurt had finally made it abate until all he felt was exhaustion.

Now he was terrified again. What if Gisele still wanted to leave?

'I can't go with you if things don't change, Emilien. I love you, with my whole heart. I don't think I'll be capable of loving anyone else the way I love you, but I want my freedom. I want my siblings in my life. But I also want to be loved and, if you can't love me and can't trust me and want to use me, then I can't be with you.'

'I know that.' He reached for her hand, taking it in both of his as he said, 'Believe me, I know that. I'm sorry that I said I couldn't love and care for you. That couldn't be further from the truth. The truth is, I think I fell in love you when you looked at me at Atelier Les Jardins. It took me a while to realise it yesterday when we were in bed together, but that's not when my feelings for you started. I trusted you for a long time, I loved you just as long, but I was trying to protect myself because I was afraid of what loving you might do to me. But, princess, I vow to you that you will have everything you want.'

'Do you mean that?'

'Yes!' He sat on the edge of the bed, dropping his elbows onto his knees. 'I was lost in my anger for so long that I couldn't let go of it, even when it was hurting me. It took you leaving to see that all I want is you.' He looked up into her warm brown eyes, hoping he could convey how desperately he wanted her. 'A life with you. It could be here in Alouette or in France; I don't care as long as we're together. I'll change my whole life for you, princess, all you have to do is say the word.'

'What about destroying the monarchy? What about Claude and Isabelle?'

'Your parents are going to answer for their crimes, which is good enough for me. Isabelle will be fine, I'm certain of it; her hulking bodyguard will accept nothing less. And, as for Claude, I think he will be a fine king.' Emilien meant every word. Many things about Gisele's brother had become clear to Emilien today.

'But what about making your father's dream a reality? You can't give up on that! I don't want you to let it all go! I want you to change the laws. I *love* that *you* want to. I know what it means to you, Emilien.'

'You mean more. I can't lose you,' he said, looking up at her.

Gisele came to him and took his hand, pulling him up.

'I can't tell you how it feels to have someone choose me above everything else. I don't have the words, but you need to know that I choose you just as completely, and we will make this happen—together. We'll make Alouette better, you and I.'

Joy. Pure joy filled his body, and he kissed her, lips pressed tightly against hers, but he didn't move. He couldn't move. His lips didn't slide against hers. They didn't rove in a passionate build to something explosive. It was desperate. He couldn't bear to part from her for the microseconds it would take to kiss, nibble and suck. It was an aching urge to cling onto her. To know she was with him—safe, entirely his and, when he finally pulled back a hair's breadth, his breath came out broken, a rough, staccato sound.

'*Mon loup*,' Gisele whispered.

'God, I want to hear that for the rest of my life.'

'You will. But first let's go home.'

EPILOGUE

Six months later

GISELE BARELY FELT the motion of the yacht out in the Mediterranean, floating somewhere between Sineaux and Saint-Lorin-de-la-Mer. She lay out on the deck on a lounger, gazing up at the sprinkling of stars in the sky, the tiny sliver of moon.

She and Emilien were on the yacht celebrating changes to the labour laws. It had taken months of work and negotiations but with Claude on their side, a new act named after Pierre Montagne had been put into law.

As soon as the parliamentary session was over, Emilien had been hounded for a statement. She'd watched on the screen in her shop as he had given one. One that he ended with, 'Now, if you'll excuse me, I need to see my wife.'

And he had come straight to her, to Atelier les Jardins, but not the one in Saint-Lorin-de-la-Mer: the one at home, in Sineaux. Gisele had opened a second shop in Alouette and already had plans to open a third, an online florist to keep up with the demand that had grown in the kingdom and in France after it was discovered the flowers were made by a princess of Alouette.

She tried to split her time between the two locations and

Emilien made that very easy to do, especially since he followed her wherever she went.

'Where you go, I go, princess,' he had said in his study one night. 'All I need is an internet connection and I can be the boss from anywhere.'

'You need to lead Montagne Holdings from your office,' she had argued.

'And yet I manage to run the company perfectly well from any country when I'm on a business trip.'

That had put an end to her worries.

As soon as Emilien entered her shop that afternoon, Gisele had seen the way he had lit up. How buoyant he seemed. The effect of years long planning had finally come to fruition. A weight off his shoulders.

She'd closed early and they had made a stop at his mother's villa, where Camille had spent an entire ocean of tears, a mix of grief, pride and happiness but mostly pride. And then they'd set sail.

On the table beside her lounger on the deck, Gisele's phone chirped with a notification and, when she checked, it was a message from Isabelle. Her sister had sent a picture of her hand on her swollen belly covered in a floral dress and the caption:

He won't be a prince. He'll be a football player.

Only if he plays for Les Phoceens, Gisele replied.

Isabelle's response was instant: Never! Sineaux FC all the way.

Gisele laughed at her sister's *faux* outrage.

'My favourite sound in the world.'

She turned to find Emilien setting two flutes filled with delicately bubbling champagne on the table beside the lounger, then he slid into the space behind her, pulling her back to his chest and framing her long legs with his powerful ones.

'It's so beautiful tonight,' she said.

'Not more beautiful than you.'

She chuckled. He told her every day how beautiful she was. He professed his love at least twice a day as if he couldn't keep it inside him, and gave her everything she wanted. She had a thriving relationship with both her siblings, the freedom to do anything she wanted and to go anywhere she wanted. The bonus was that she had Emilien's unequivocal support through it all.

'Who were you chatting to?' he asked. She felt the rumble of his low voice against her back.

'Isabelle. The baby's being active.' She threaded her fingers through Emilien's. 'She'll be the perfect mother. She's already a perfect princess.'

'Do you wish we had made different decisions?'

She and Emilien had already made an official announcement that they were stepping down from active royal duties. But she could hear in his voice that, if she changed her mind, he would follow her lead and make royal life a dream she'd never known it could be.

'No. I never wanted to be a princess; I just wanted to be happy. You make me happy.'

'You make me happy too, Gisele.'

His arms tightened around her as he kissed her neck. Emilien had given her everything he promised but he'd given her one additional thing. The one thing he hadn't wanted to promise to anyone. His love.

* * * * *

*Did you fall in love with
Princess Bride with Benefits?
Then make sure to check out the next instalment
in the Scandals at the Palace trilogy, coming soon.
In the meantime, explore these other stories by
Bella Mason!*

Their Diamond Ring Ruse
His Chosen Queen
Strictly Forbidden Boss
Pregnant Before 'I Do'
Snowed-In Enemies

Available now!

Get up to 4 Free Books!

We'll send you 2 free books from each series you try
PLUS a free Mystery Gift.

Both the **Harlequin Presents** and **Harlequin Medical Romance** series
feature exciting stories of passion and drama.

YES! Please send me 2 FREE novels from Harlequin Presents or Harlequin Medical Romance and my FREE gift (gift is worth about $10 retail). I may cancel anytime by emailing ReaderServiceInfo@Harlequin.com or by calling 1-800-873-8635.If I don't cancel, I will receive 6 brand-new larger-print novels every month and be billed just $7.19 each in the U.S., or $7.99 each in Canada, or 4 brand-new Harlequin Medical Romance Larger-Print books every month and be billed just $7.19 each in the U.S. or $7.99 each in Canada. That's a savings of 20% off the cover price! It's quite a bargain! Shipping and handling is just 75¢ per book in the U.S. and $1.75 per book in Canada.* I understand that accepting the free books and gift places me under no obligation to buy anything—they are mine to keep for free no matter what I decide.

Choose one: ☐ **Harlequin Presents Larger-Print** (176/376 BPA G3CD) ☐ **Harlequin Medical Romance** (171/371 BPA G3CD) ☐ **Or Try Both!** (176/376 & 171/371 BPA G3CE)

Name (please print)

Address   Apt. #

City   State/Province   Zip/Postal Code

Email: Please check this box ☐ if you would like to receive newsletters and promotional emails from Harlequin Enterprises ULC and its affiliates. You can unsubscribe anytime.

Mail to the **Harlequin Reader Service:**
IN U.S.A.: P.O. Box 1341, Buffalo, NY 14240-8531
IN CANADA: P.O. Box 603, Fort Erie, Ontario L2A 5X3

Want to explore our other series or interested in ebooks? Visit www.ReaderService.com or call 1-800-873-8635.

*Terms and prices subject to change without notice. Prices do not include sales taxes, which will be charged (if applicable) based on your state or country of residence. Canadian residents will be charged applicable taxes. Offer not valid in Quebec. This offer is limited to one order per household. Books received may not be as shown. Not valid for current subscribers to the Harlequin Presents or Harlequin Medical Romance series. All orders subject to approval. Credit or debit balances in a customer's account(s) may be offset by any other outstanding balance owed by or to the customer. Please allow 4 to 6 weeks for delivery. Offer available while quantities last.

Your Privacy — Your information is being collected by Harlequin Enterprises ULC, operating as Harlequin Reader Service. For a complete summary of the information we collect, how we use this information and to whom it is disclosed, please visit our privacy notice located at https://corporate.harlequin.com/privacy-notice. Notice to California Residents—Under California law, you have specific rights to control and access your data. For more information on these rights and how to exercise them, visit https://corporate.harlequin.com/california-privacy. For additional information for residents of other U.S. states that provide their residents with certain rights with respect to personal data, visit https://corporate.harlequin.com/other-state-residents-privacy-rights.

HPHM2603